The Drunk Detective

The Drunk Detective

Mary Jean Curry

PRODIGY GOLD BOOKS

PHILADELPHIA * LOS ANGELES

THE DRUNK DETECTIVE

A Prodigy Gold Book

Prodigy Gold E-book edition/March 2018

Prodigy Gold Paperback edition/March 2018

Copyright (c) 2018 by Rahiem Brooks

Library of Congress Catalog Card Number: 2017944620

Website: http://www.prodigygoldbooks.com

Author's e-mail: authormaryjeancurry@gmail.com

This novel is a work of fiction. Any references to real people, event, business, organization, or locales are intended only to give the fiction a sense of reality and authenticity. Names, characters, place, and incidents are the product of the author's imagination or used fictitiously. Any resemblance to actual persons, living or dead, events, or locales, is entirely coincidental.

All rights reserved. No parts of this book may be used or reproduced in any manner whatsoever without written permission from the author, except in case of brief quotations embodied in critical articles and reviews.

ISBN 978-1-939665-00-3

Published simultaneously in the US and Canada

PRINTED IN THE UNITED STATES OF AMERICA

For Ben Matlock and Sherlock Holmes

The Drunk Detective

CHAPTER 1

Refer to her as Dotty.

Better yet, don't refer to her for any reason, and definitely if it's not about money. Calling her before noon, despite her profession, was also out of the question. If you do she's undoubtedly going to answer on the fourth ring and say something like: "I don't know you and your call may be important, but at this time it's not. Please, do the police a favor, hang up right now, or I will hunt you down and drain your car's brake fluid."

The caller sighed. "Too bad I don't own a car."

"Then I'll do something of remarkable relevance to you in the eyes of a coroner."

"Look, is this, Dotty?"

The voice was a low seductive one made for late night radio. Quite smooth. The last thing she wanted to hear was some catty woman at this hour. "Who the hell's calling?"

THE DRUNK DETECTIVE

"Frankie, ma'am."

"Doesn't ring a bell."

"Frankie Robinson. I live in the apartment right below you, for crying out loud. We speak every day."

"The male stripper? Sometimes gigolo?"

"Um, Dotty, you live over a Chinese owned massage parlor known to give happy endings. What do you expect for a neighbor, a damn neurosurgeon?"

Dotty sat up in her twin-sized bed and ran a hand through her elephant-colored hair. Her hair was course and dry. She fished around her nightstand and found a Mickey Mouse watch. She angled it to see its face using the light making its way into her bedroom from the massage parlor's outside signage. She sat the watch down and whined into the receiver, "It's three-thirty a-damn-m."

"Gee, all of my clocks stopped, so I called you for the time. Thanks. Look, you're some kind of detective lady, correct?"

"Not at this time of the morning."

"I'll give you five-hundred bucks to come down to my apartment right now."

She drew a deep breath. "Shouldn't I be offering you money?"

"What the fuck, Dotty. Can you come down or not? You ain't the only detective with breasts in town. I only called you because you could get here the quickest."

"What's your problem? You have to have one."

"As a matter of fact, I do have a dead nun in my bed. And Dotty that is a huge fuckin' problem."

* * *

When the he-bitch repeated himself, she said that she was heading right down and hung up. She sat there and ran her tongue across her front teeth. They felt like they were covered in dust. When she threw back her blanket, a round brandy bottle popped into the air. She tried catching it, but realized it was empty, and let it drop to the floor. She slipped on tattered slippers and ambled to a cluttered bathroom, which wasn't going to change. She plopped on the toilet to empty her bladder, while engaged in her morning routine, asking herself:

"What's your name? Dorothy Davis."

"And where do you live? I don't freakin' know."

"Where did you drink last night? Oh, come on."

One out of three wasn't bad. Hell, that was better than usual.

Back in the bedroom she fell onto the bed and pulled her hair into a sloppy ponytail and after scanning the floor she found a pair of jeans. These she slipped over pink cotton pajamas, which peeked out at the bottom of her pant legs. She slid on Christmas themed argyle socks and pushed them into penny loafers with dimes in them. It was February so she tugged on a puffy jacket, grunting with the effort. She was fifty-six, overweight, strong as a bull. She looked for her semi-automatic simply because it was 3:30 a.m. in downtown Philadelphia, but she was wasting her time; she hadn't seen it in weeks. She forgot about it and headed out. The hallway smelled of incense, condoms, and collard greens.

Frankie Robinson's buzzer actually worked. None of the other tenants did, and the landlord didn't care one iota. The door creaked open. Frankie's head was just below the top of the door frame. He was shirtless in red boxer briefs and neat dreadlocks rested on his shoulders.

THE DRUNK DETECTIVE

"You look ridiculous," he said.

"I'm running on three hours sleep. I see why the ladies love you, though. Where's my five hundred?"

"Don't you want to see the body first?"

"Hell no. Do I look like a lesbian?"

"Don't make me answer that." They stepped away from the doorway and he removed a painting from the wall revealing a safe. He opened it, pulled out some cash and pushed five hundred into Dotty's palm. He put the rest back, locked the safe and replaced the painting.

"I thought you kept your money in the nightstand where the broads leave it for you after sordid sex." She scanned the bills and then pocketed them.

"Funny. Mine is hidden for creeps like you that think they know everything."

He locked the front door and led her through a cramped living room styled by an IKEA rep into a tiny bedroom containing a queen-sized water bed that took up ninety-percent of the room. The other ten was occupied by Sister Anne Tudor, principal of Our Lady of Rosary, the Catholic school that prepared her daughter for college.

For the first time she saw the sister's curves sans her religious habits. Mother Superior's face was rosy and her mouth was curved into a smile. She died happy.

Dotty fished into her jacket pocket for a toothpick and stuck it into her mouth. She twirled it around and was beginning to feel better already. "She a constant client?"

"Loose lips, sinks my future. I don't kiss and report it. I thought that she was breathing heavy. Then she wasn't at all."

"Welp, she's deader'n Mother Theresa."

"Once again, thank you. I thought she was mimicking a fucking BMW."

"At least she's no lesbo." She tossed a hand on her lips. "Let me guess, you have no idea where I was at last night do you?"

He furrowed his brow and slapped a hand on her shoulder. "You wouldn't be up if you had been here, Dotty. I assure you."

"I'll recall soon enough. What do you actually want me to do?"

"Get her the hell out of here, what else? Cops find a nun's body here, I'll lose my nicely set up tax-free enterprise."

"Five more hundred."

"Get the fuck outta here. I just gave you five bills."

"So. That was to show my pretty face. You're lucky I don't charge by the pound. Look at those hips and that gut. Geesh."

"{You} look the hell at it. She's on her back because she liked it missionary. I had to climb on that."

"And you call this a nice enterprise. You're shitten me. What's five more hundred? You don't even flash your beef for that."

"You're a real comedian."

"So I've been told."

He walked out of the room and came back with five more hundred. She didn't count the money this time. "You need to leave for a while," she said. "Come back when the sun breaks with breakfast for two."

"Where the hell am I going this late?"

"Pick a bed. Any bed. Give yours a break for a change. Go to a cocaine club. What? Am I a vacation planner? Use your brain for something besides giving brain."

"Son of a bitch." He ran his thumbs in the waist of his boxer briefs about to remove them, stopped. "You just going to stare at me? I only wore these for the sister."

"Is there a problem? Oh, payment. I'm broke."

"Get the hell out, lady."

"You should have told the nun that, before she died under you."

She got the hell out, slamming the bedroom door shut. In the living room, still working the toothpick, she drifted to the painting and removed it from the wall. The safe was locked. Frankie, in white boxers and a tank top, came out of the bedroom carrying a gun, put the painting back on the wall, and said, "I will kill you 'bout my money, Dotty." She admired his backside as he walked back into the bedroom.

Ten minutes later he emerged wearing jeans and a sweater that clung to his muscles. He was a dark skinned man, under thirty with boyish looks that authorized him to tell clients that he was nineteen. Cougars liked him young. He had a special trick that he did with his goatee that they liked also. Something about the way he handled himself made her wish she was a MILF.

"So where to?"

"A client's house. Gotta make my thousand bucks back by sunrise to be able to afford to bring you breakfast." He stopped at the front door. "What are you going to do with her?"

"Don't ask. You didn't want to tell me your dealings with her."

"Fuck you."

"Go fuck yourself."

When he had gone, she helped herself to a bottled Corona beer from the 'fridge in the kitchen. She drank another while looking up a number in her cell phone, as she headed back to the bedroom. She sat on the edge of the bed while waiting for someone to answer her call. She tapped the bed. "So, Sister. He worth the money?"

"You better believe it, honey."

Dotty spit out the toothpick, as the phone continued to ring. She cleared her throat. "Is this Our Lady of the Rosary parish?"

"Yes, this is Bishop Sinclair. It's four, you know?"

"Thank you. The name's Dorothy Davis. I'm a private dick, I mean, detective. I'm sorry."

"You should be."

"I'm also sorry to inform you that Sister Tudor is dead."

"Jesus Christ." The irritation left his voice. "How? What happened?"

"I'm not a doctor. But I think it's heart related."

"Virgin Mary Mother of God. In bed?"

"How'd you guess?" She held back inappropriate laughter.

"Was she...Could she have been in a state of grace?"

Dotty pulled out another toothpick. "Now you see why I'm calling at four a.m., Bishop Sinclair," she said and added, "we really need to talk."

MARY JEAN CURRY

CHAPTER 2

What a place to die. "It had better been worth it." When she was through chastising the nun, she phoned the massage parlor downstairs. It rang and rang until a voice like gravel being ground picked up.

"What the hell. Hello."

"Chen, this is Dotty."

"So. It's four thirty a.m."

"Appreciate it. I'm up at Frankie's sex room."

"Must be nice?" There was a chuckle in his voice.

"I need to borrow your camera. It records, too, right?"

Pause. "Who you going to get to take the shots of you two? I sure as hell ain't."

"Cut it out. Bring it up to me."

"Um. What about the back rent?"

"I have two hundred for you right now. I just need to borrow the camera."

"You should also give me whatever you planned on paying the play boy horse. Besides, the last time you borrowed something I saw it at a pawn shop."

"It was swiped from my car. How many times we have to go over this?"

"You pawning something of mine, missing or being late with my rent due dates the last twelve years or more?"

"Look its to early. I need the camera."

"Use your cell phone."

"Can't. It's a dated flip phone. You going to give it to me or not?"

"Frankie's giving it to you."

"Sad."

"You got five hundred bucks?"

"Hell no. The camera isn't even worth that much."

"Already thinking of how much you can sell it for, eh?"

"No, man."

"OK, you have two hundred cash?"

"Yes, what you think I was going to use my Amex Black Card?"

"Just checking. Last time you wrote me a check, it bounced from here to Shangai. My father caught it there."

"Chen."

"I'll be up. Have the cash in your greasy palms."

Dotty hung up. Conversations with her landlord was like playing tennis in a fish bowl. Without thought she pocketed an expensive watch she found on the night stand.

Chen sounded like a NFL commentator and looked like a house in a town called Pleasantville with his neatness. He was anything but. He had an emaciated square frame, perfectly bald head, bold eyes, a square nose, and when he walked his feet pointed outward like a penguin's. Old age had claimed his hair; Dotty had a bet with a bookie that Chen had a bald crotch, but neither had had any real motivation to find out to win the bet. He stood in the hallway wearing a lint covered pajama set and dangling the camera, a new Polaroid, from its strap at his side. "My money?"

Dotty had the two hundred separated from her eight and laid two in the landlord's skinny palm.

"I don't know where you got the loot. But before you spend it all tricking, remember you owe me six more hundred."

"Give me this."

He gave it to her. "Where's the horse?"

"Out. Working."

"I thought this was a home based business? No?"

"Not right now." Dotty turned on the camera. "You didn't see me head out last night, did you?"

"Watched you go and return. It was after midnight. You look ridiculous, by the way."

"Did I return with anyone?"

"Yes, as a matter of fact you did. Kat William and Kevin Hart. How could you forget their company? The lucky charm pimp and chocolate drop the rapper."

THE DRUNK DETECTIVE

She hung her head low. "Good night, Chen. I'll return this later."

"You do that. I think I should come in and look around. It ain't like Frankie to be out this time of the morning. He could get raped by some crazy broad."

Dotty stepped in front of the door. "That would be theft of services. Get lost Chen. And don't forget to credit me the deuce."

Chen left and Dotty closed the door and locked it. She went through the photos on the camera and found salacious photos of the mayor and his mistress on several dates entering and exiting several suburban hotels. She had planned on making a buck off the sale of the photos to the mayor's wife, but she died of cancer rendering the photos worthless. She hated the city's corrupt politicians and sought to bring them all down on her spare time.

In the bedroom, she turned on the bedroom's overhead light and a bedside lamp illuminating Sister Tudor's bloated countenance. Her plumpness looked as if she was crying out loud in the confessional. Opening the closet, Dotty flipped through the clothing hanging there. Nothing suited what she looked for. She opened a drawer of the dresser and found several underwear types. She pulled out leopard print boxer briefs with Monday embroidered on the ass. She stepped back to survey the bed and then surmised the scene was too stuffy. She tossed the briefs on the bedpost with the day prominently displayed.

"There you go."

She took a series of pictures from many angles, finishing the photo shoot from the top of the bed that made the Sister look like an oversized Mona Lisa, then put the camera in her back pocket and went back to her apartment to stash it. Chen could take her to Judge Judy for it.

Back at Frankie's she put away her underwear prop, just then the door buzzer sounded.

"Dorothy Davis?"

The man ducked his head as he entered the apartment, with a complexion like damp clay and hair as white as snow, cropped close to his scalp. His feet were as huge as his hands with chewed-off fingernails. His black trench coat was dull.

"Yeah. You've been sent by the Bishop?"

"I'm Lynch."

The bishop had given him that name, and it may not have been real. She stepped aside and the tall man went straight to the bedroom without looking at anything else. Once there he looked at every aspect of the room.

"Awfully bright."

"I'm not used to being in the dark with a corpse," Dotty said.

"I have a time or two. Is there a fire escape?"

"Yup, but I doubt its been used since the Regan era. That's how long I've been living here. I wouldn't try to access it carrying a dead nun."

Lynch continued to admire the body. "She's bigger than I thought."

"You bring a dolly?"

"No." He lifted the nun's naked leg from the bed and let it drop. "Let's get her clothed while she's still flexible."

"You sound like a professional dead body remover. Why should we waste time dressing her?"

THE DRUNK DETECTIVE

"It makes perfect sense to carry a naked body down two flights of stairs."

"Yeah, you must be a pro. What is it that you do for the bishop again?"

"I never said. The fee was three hundred." Dotty coughed up the money from her bra. A frosty hand touched Dotty's as the bills changed hands.

"Well let's do this."

The canoness' clothes consisted of black lace panties with a matching bra worn under her black tunic. She wore rosary beads around her neck. Lynch got the deceased left arm into a bra strap and, mumbling, lifted the upper body by the shoulders for Dotty to manage the other side. The nun groaned.

Dotty jumped to the other side of the room, slamming into the dresser. "She's alive!"

"That's just some left over air trapped in her lungs. They often do that. Hold her torso up, so I can slip on her panties." Next he covered her head and hair in her veil and coif.

Dotty apprehensively helped.

A half hour later passed before the nun was dressed and Dotty exchanged her disgust for exhaustion. They got her dressed, and then both put on a shoe and tied the laces.

Dotty dropped onto the bed and wiped her brow with her shirt sleeve. "If only my mother could see me. She always encouraged me to be closer to the Church."

"Top or bottom?"

She looked at Lynch, who still had on his coat, buttoned all the way up. "Do you sweat?"

"I wasn't paid for that. It'll be daybreak soon."

"Yes, and I have breakfast coming."

Dotty took the head. They smoothly got the dead body into the hallway, and dragged it's heels across the runner onto the staircase landing, where they stood it against the wall. An old woman appeared at the bottom of the stairs, and started up carrying a handbag the size of Canada.

Dotty, kept the nun stable with a hand under her arm, smiled. "Good morning, Mrs. Lombardo. How was the casino?"

"I won, Dotty," she said two steps from the landing. "Every now and then Sugar House lets someone win. Who's that with you?"

"Just my buddy and his savior."

"She looks to need saving. She can barely stand up. My lips are sealed, because I don't like when the media airs out the Church's dirty laundry. I can understand a girl needing a drink, though. Don't let her drive."

"We're not, Mrs. Lombardo."

"She looks tore up from the floor up. Dead, in fact. She should've ate before drinking."

Dotty offered a strained smile. "Well, good night, Mrs. Lombardo."

"Good night, boys. And remember she can't drive." She continued to her apartment and locked herself inside.

"Mrs. Lombardo," Dotty told Lynch. "She was wasted herself."

"Think she's on to us?"

"She won't even recall this encounter in an hour."

"OK, let's get the Sister to the car. Give me a hand."

THE DRUNK DETECTIVE

"Can't we just drag her down?"

"No. She'll get postmortem marks."

"Smart. Once again I ask, what do you do for the bishop." She began to be worried about her own well being and wished she had her gun.

The nun was stiffening. Dotty put her in a full-Nelson wrestling move--saying, "Lord, forgive me"--and, bearing a lot of weight backed down the stairs while Lynch held the feet in the air from snagging the heels on the shabby staircase runner. They stopped three times to rest. Dotty's nose was in Sister Tudor's collar for the trip down the stairs, long enough for her to develop a disdain for Chanel No. 5.

Just off the second landing, her foot slipped. She began to fall over, tried using the wall for leverage, managed to smash herself between the wall and her problem, said, "Jesus!" and let the nun go.

"Catch her, idiot." Lynch barked. Dotty caught her.

Executing a perfect curtsy, the nun tipped forward down the stairwell with Dotty embracing her from the back. They fell down the steps and landed in the tiled foyer, coming to rest against the door that led to the vestibule and sidewalk.

Lynch leaped down the stairs. "Great catch."

Dotty, sprawled on top of the corpse, said, "Now I have a damn pre-mortem bruise."

CHAPTER 3

The car parked in front of the massage parlor's front door was a charcoal gray Cadillac; a big one mirroring a hearse. She stood in the doorway holding up the body while Lynch checked the street. She sighed and wished this whole ordeal was over with.

"Let's do it." Lynch was gaunt and barely alive as the nun under the dim light in the foyer. "Put her on the front passenger side."

"Huh? Why not the back seat? Lay her right across it."

"Because then it'll actually look like a dead nun and not a sleeping one. You sure you're a detective?"

"Hell, let's put her behind the wheel. That'll be fun."

The passenger door was opened and they both tossed an arm on their shoulders and walked across the sidewalk--Dotty losing more breath with each step--sat her on the seat, got her feet inside, and positioning her upright before securing the seat belt, pulling it to its limits.

"Just marvelous." Dotty's voice was a high-pitched soprano.

"Make sure she doesn't go any where while I run upstairs to be sure everything is in order."

"Where the fucks she goin'? Opps. Sorry Sister."

"Just wait here. I can't believe this." Lynch went inside.

The night air was cold and whipping trash around the filthy downtown street. Dotty closed the nun's door and went around the back to sit in the driver's seat, closing the door. After a second or two, she let down the window. "You really splashed on the perfume tonight, honey." Just at that moment a police officer walked around the corner doing his rounds. The massage parlor was close to the Philadelphia Convention Center and its patrons were known to be robbed so police patrolled the area on foot for suspicious activity.

Dotty said O-fuck and looked for the car's keys, while sliding down in the seat. No such luck. The officer came over and shone a flashlight in her face.

"Does there seem to be a problem, ma'am?"

Dotty sat up. "No problem at all, sir. I'm just waiting on someone, he forgot his coat. Sir."

The officer shifted his flashlight past Dotty, who became moist under her armpits. "Ma'am is your other friend asleep or passed out?"

"Oh, this is my aunt June. I had to pick up my friend and was forced to bring her along so she wouldn't be left home alone. She's known to start fires."

The flashlight's angle shifted. Dotty leaned forward, then sat upright when the officer moved it out of her face. The beam shifted to the dead nun again, then darted back to Dotty, then back to the nun and rested there a long time.

"Does she need a doctor, ma'am? Is she a nun?"

"No and no sir, Officer, sir. She's schizophrenic and sometimes thinks she's a member of the Church. The meds had her knocked out cold. I told you she gets violent and starts fires if we don't dress her like this."

"Ma'am, are you being an ass by making fun of me by keep calling me, sir?"

"No, sir. I mean no. But you keep calling me ma'am. Just saying."

The officer shook his head. He was in his forties, with a square jaw and rough moustache and dull green eyes under the square visor of his cap.

"Wake her," he said.

"Please don't make me do that." She resisted another {sir.}

"No, I said wake her up. If you even can, 'cause she looks dead to my trained eye."

"Dead?" Dotty gave the officer a tortured grin. "Dead that's a good one. Ha-ha, dead."

"I wanna hear her laugh."

"Trust me, she lost her sense of humor when JFK was killed. That's what sent her over to the crazy side."

"Oh, really." The officer stepped back a few inches and groped his pistol. "Step out of the vehicle, ma'am."

Dotty had a terrible idea. Here goes nothing, she thought.

She slid her right arm behind the dead woman's back, saying, "Look alive, June. We're back home." She pushed the corpse's top half forward toward the dashboard. It moaned.

THE DRUNK DETECTIVE

The officer chilled out, and took his hand off of his weapon.

"My apologies, ma'am. We have to be vigilant in the neighborhood. There are many weirdoes. No offense, ma'am."

"Yes, sir. I mean no sir. I mean no." Dotty had a firm grip on the nun's coat to keep her head from slamming into the dash. "I agree that you can't be to careful."

"It's just to protect us. You better get out of this area. She sounded awful."

"Yes sir."

"It's five-thirty a.m., you know?"

"Thanks, Officer."

The officer went on his merry way. Dotty let go of the nun and tossed a new toothpick in her mouth. Lynch appeared from the building with a sneer on his face.

"My God, what took you so long? A damn cop was here." Dotty got out of the car.

"I watched him. He smell a crime?"

"At first. I handled him, though. I gotta tell you, I haven't spent this much time with the clergy since I was baptized."

"You were raised a Christian?"

"My mother and father were devout Evangelicals. You know the ones all of the Republicans fight over for the presidential nomination. My husband tried converting me to the Catholic faith. It didn't take."

"Where is he now?"

"Alabama or Arkansas, or maybe it was Alaska. Definitely an {A} state."

"Divorced?"

"By now. I hope so. I'd hate to die and he get half of my apartment."

Lynch climbed into the driver's seat. "I guess this is where we say goodbye."

"What you plan to do with her?"

"You don't really even care."

"Lynch, I've known people fifteen years that I haven't been around this damn long."

"Well, it's over now." He slammed the door.

"Look, I'll keep it quiet."

Lynch started the engine. "What?"

"I said I'll keep quiet."

"Good for you." He rolled up the window and began to dial a number into his cell phone.

Dotty raced up to her apartment and took up position in her window to be sure that Lynch left with the nun. She watched him pull off and bend around the corner. She wondered if she should have waved goodbye; to Sister Tudor, not Lynch.

She had to be to work at nine a.m., but she wasn't tired any more. She played with the camera and looked at her handy work. She connected it to her computer and downloaded the pictures into a locked folder. The watch that she purloined from Frankie was a Rolex that she stuck in a desk drawer where she kept a bag of marijuana.

Yawning now, she curled up in bed at six a.m. and was feeling better. Her hangover had subdued--although she didn't recall where she had gotten wasted the night before--she had five hundred dollars extra cash in her pocket, and pictures of a dead Catholic nun in a gigolo's bed. This was a great morning.

She woke up when a burly white fireman chopped through her apartment door with an axe.

"Where the hell is the fire?" asked the rookie fireman.

Dotty shot up and ran fingers through her hair. "That's my damn line."

"Wrong floor, Adam," someone yelled from the hallway. "Some prostitute's apartment below this one."

"My bad about the door ma'am." Adam ran out.

Dotty said, "Fuck" and looked for her jeans.

CHAPTER 4

The arson investigator's name was Rodriguez.

His suit was blue and he had sweat running from his forehead that he kept wiping with a sooty handkerchief that left smudges. He was much smaller than the fireman that had chopped down Dotty's door and a couple of years younger than her. He wrapped a petite hand with blackened nails around Dotty's hand in greeting and ushered her out of the fried hallway into Frankie Robinson's apartment. To Dotty's dismay he lit a cigarette, dropped the match on the floor and the carpet smoldered.

What an idiot, she thought.

"Too much smoke in here."

"You don't say," she replied. "Smells like a bar-b-cue."

He blew smoke rings into the air.

"That would be the tenant. Know him at all?"

"We spoke on occasion. He OK?"

THE DRUNK DETECTIVE

"At this point he should be getting worked on at the Burn Center of University of Penn Hospital in West Philly. They work miracles of Godly proportions there."

Perhaps, Sister Tudor was already an angel and looking over him, Dotty wished she could blurt.

"What's he do for a living?"

"Hook. What happened, I smell gas?"

"Could be that. He have any clients lately, well, last night?"

"That's how he gets the money to pay for the gas and other necessities, I presume."

"Can you describe any from last night?"

"I don't look at the broads. I hear them sometimes. The walls are thin. One of them could be the mayor's wife or something."

"What about any loud disturbances? You do live right above him."

"All arguments are loud, don't you think?" She fished in her pocket for a toothpick and found none. She pulled out her box of matchsticks to substitute, but thought better of it, given the company. "You think this was a purposeful act? Like someone tried to kill, Frankie?"

Rodriguez wiped his forehead. "Don't know the motive. You've been no help, Ms. Davis."

"You should be talking to Chen, the landlord. It's not my job to help you. You're the arson guru."

"I've talked to Chen. He was just as useless. By the way what is your job?"

"Private dick."

"Interesting. Than I'm sure you've paid far more attention to what's going on around here than you're letting on. You with an agency, or are you a loner like Dick Tracey?" He casually tapped live ashes onto the carpet. There was a little flame there, Dotty stamped out.

"Fuck Dick Tracey. He's fictional, sir. I work for Goldberg Discreet Inquirers on Broad and Arch Streets. I got to be there in a half hour." She had spent an hour in the hallway with other residents, watching firemen put out the fire and paramedics carry Frankie Robinson out covered in a white sheet. Chen found him balled into the fetal position on the wall opposite his apartment door, where the blast had shot him when he'd come home. Two platters of food lay beside him. Dotty was touched and had slept right through the explosion and the ensuing sirens. "And to be clear, if some nut job is blowing up my neighbors, I am privileged to the information."

"We've got no reason to believe that. I investigate arson leading to death. Does Frankie Robinson smoke?"

"He is now."

Rodriguez wiped his forehead, dropped the cigarette butt on the floor, and put away his tape recorder. "OK, that's all, I guess. Can I get a number to reach you?"

Dotty dug into her pocket and pulled out a few cards and gave him one engraved on red stock with a bouquet of white and yellow roses in the corner. The arson investigator furrowed his eyebrows. "A woman started the agency," Dotty said.

"Thanks for your time, Ms. Davis." Rodriguez opened the door for her.

Dotty left after stomping on the cigarette butt still smoking on the floor.

Dotty made her way back to the fourth floor and before she could get into her apartment Chen was on the fourth floor landing. With his hands in the pockets of his fuzzy pajamas and the dull hallway light shining on him.

"Not so fast, Dotty. What was you moving downstairs this morning after I gave you the camera, a load of bowling balls?" he asked.

Dotty expected the question to come from the arson investigator. "I had fell after slipping on that dated runner. You need to replace it."

"Where's your bruises? You had to have something break your fall."

"You sound like a cop. I have to get to work, Chen."

"Speaking of cops, I didn't tell the cops that you was the last person I saw in Frankie's place."

"Why not? The doll has not committed no crime."

"My camera?"

She covered her mouth and raised her eyebrows. "You know what. Funny story. It was in my car..."

"Look at this catastrophe." Chen was looking at the smoke covered walls. "I don't have money to redo these walls and my insurance won't cover arson unless someone is arrested and convicted for it. The cop's running around here are messing with the parlor's flow of traffic. People are discouraged from coming."

Dotty nodded. What could she say.

"Yup, that was a loud noise you made this morning with your skinny friend. I saw him," the landlord continued. He was now whispering. "I thought it was burglars, but I got a good view of you two through my peephole, Dotty. You were right on top of it. I hope I never get that huge."

"Look, get to the point, Chen."

"I'm old, not dumb. It was easy for me to put together an unknown man and a camera and a gigolo and a dead person dressed like a nun on the stairs. It'd be easy for the police, too. They tie those facts with the explosion and you have a problem bigger than any client you've ever had at Goldberg's."

"Arson crew called it a gas leak."

"And they may continue to believe that if you catch my drift."

"Chen, I don't get the drift at all."

"You got till tonight to get it. That's all the time I'll forget to give the cops these details. I want half your action, that's all I want. What's half? You decide and find me to discuss. You know I'm always here just like I was this morning. The peephole's a marvelous invention."

"I'm late for work, Chen."

Chen stepped out of her way. "Work won't matter if you're in jail, Dotty."

Dotty E-mailed the pictures to herself before heading out of her apartment and to work. She then changed her computer password and hid the camera. She didn't trust Chen and his key to her apartment.

* * *

The car she drove to work was a brand-new Mercedes S-series with cream guts. It belonged to a judge friend who had asked Dotty to sell it for her while she served a five-year sentence for taking bribes to alter criminal trial outcomes, only Dotty hadn't made time to sell it. The morning was the color of granite which matched the color of the over cast clouds, and the sun may not have been up. As she zipped around cars and pedestrians barely missing both, she thought about the explosion at Frankie's apartment. Although the building had had leaks in the past, she kept wondering what Lynch did for the bishop and what had he done during that lonely trip back up to the apartment without Dotty. {Coincidence, that's all a dick hopes for to close a file,} he mentor, old Donna Goldberg had said once. {When you record a man walking out of a house carrying a gasoline can and then the house goes up in flames, that check is as good as yours.} Except in that case the man with the can was a state representative and his wife was inside; which {had} been an accident. It had taken ten-thousand-dollars to stop the state rep from pressing charges for Dotty trespassing and leaking the footage to the local media. Regardless, it was sound advice.

Continuing her deep thoughts about the eruption, Dotty parked in a loading zone in front of the building on Broad Street and spent some time deciding which placard she wanted to prominently display in her window to avoid a ticket and tow. She selected VISITING CLERGY and said, "How appropriate," before she went into the building.

The gold letters on the wood doors to the floor where she worked read Goldberg Discreet Inquirers. The receptionist desk was shaped like a horseshoe and behind it was a male secretary who was really a guard in position to stop any crazies from coming in killing the investigator that exposed them. The glass coffee table was topped with spy and mystery magazines and paintings of fictional detectives covered the walls. It was an impressive sight which Dotty barely appreciated. She liked the old drab style before the makeover with PRESTIGE DETECTIVE AGENCY painted on the door.

The receptionist was in a tight suit and his muscles were about to pop the threads.

"Morning, Jack," Dotty said. "You ought to lay off the steroids and performance enhancement drugs. I can imagine how small your phallus has gotten."

He didn't look up from the Philadelphia Daily News. "Mr. Goldberg wants you in his office."

"What he want this time around, my luscious body?"

"Just your heart. He asked me to send in the dickhead as soon as she shows up."

"You're kidding right? How'd you assume he meant me?"

"This agency is like a pair of trousers. Only one dickhead can fit in them at a time." He turned the page.

She smiled and leaned into him, whispering, "The Roosevelt Inn rents by the hour. How 'bout it?"

He finally looked up from the newspaper, frowned, and gave her a look to kill. "How 'bout a sexual harassment charge?"

"Gym rats. Never a direct answer." She shrugged and went through the door behind the desk.

She meandered down the short hallway fixing her clothes along the way. A cheap, barely pressed, business suit didn't do much for her personality but it was the attire for the office. She checked her hair in a wall mirror, which was out of the ponytail and a strategic mess before she knocked on the bosses door. She was wearing her lucky ascot, an expensive Versace number left in the glove box of her judge friend's car. She was serving time, so had no need for it.

"Come in, Dotty."

THE DRUNK DETECTIVE

The office was huge and decorated with a masculine tone, black carpet, white walls, and a glass desk. A few awards were on the walls and windows on the south and west sides looked out on Arch and Broad Streets. On his desk was a framed photo of his dead wife who had started the agency with desires to be a dominate female private eye.

"Rumor has it that you wanted to see me, Mr. Goldberg?"

"I did at nine, but as usual you're late."

"There was a fire, well, and explosion in my apartment building. I could've died." She clutched her heart.

"I had thought maybe your brother was sick again. Do you have a brother, Dotty?"

"He's on death row in a state prison. Him and my dad had a flare up, a carving knife got involved. Last Thanksgiving dinner my family ever shared."

The agency's owner was sitting at his desk staring out of the window at the statute of Ben Franklin on the top of City Hall. He was the same height as Dotty but in great shape for early sixties. He wore contacts most times and cheap suits paired with clip-on ties. He finally looked at Dotty and frowned.

"Tell me about this morning, ma'am?"

"The fire? What about it?"

"Before the fire."

Dotty wanted to run. She reached into her pocket for a toothpick and couldn't find one. She wondered how many people watched her ushering a dead nun to a car.

"This morning, you mean?" she asked.

"You're playing games. This morning, last night, you know what the hell I mean. When people with jobs to report to in the a.m. are sleeping. Just what do you think you were doing?"

"You've talked to Bishop Sinclair?"

"Who? You thought it best to jeopardize your job by calling me just after midnight asking about who I sleep with?"

"Who me?"

Luscious Goldberg spun in his chair and stood up. He got up close to Dotty, and clear gray eyes stared deeply at her. "Let me help jog your vodka-fogged memory since amnesia is your defense. Let's play dumb-dumb games. I don't appreciate you waking me up asking if I sleep with a blow up doll."

"Who did that?" She resisted the urge to laugh.

"You claimed to have a bet with a guy at the bar."

"Oh my. Did I tell you the name of the bar?"

"That's besides the point. What you do on your time is your business, thank the Lord, but when you involve me in your off the wall antics, I will put my foot so far up your ass, you'll cough up shoe polish."

"I was white girl wasted."

"I wouldn't know you sober. That's part of the problem. No more drinking on my clock. That's a new rule, you got that?"

"Oh, come on. I meet clients at bars. They're depressed. We drink. It wouldn't be polite for me not to drink with them."

"Dotty, there's always a pint of gin in your desk trash can and a fifth of vodka in your car's arm rest and I bet you have a flask in your left pocket right now. You're a walking speakeasy. If a client invites you to drink, give them their money back. I hope that's loud and clear.

"Goldberg does inquirers," he added. "That means employee thefts, criminal background checks, look for missing teens. No divorces. No peeking in peepholes. And we do not photograph or blackmail adulterers."

"Yes, sir."

"When my wife died, her will demanded that I keep you on staff and I don't know what she liked about you. There's nothing to like. But I am prepared to have my lawyers help me break my wife's will to toss you into the streets on your big ass. Last night's little call almost had me there. You got that?"

"Yes, sir."

"You say, 'Yes sir,' but I bet you're really thinking, 'to hell with you asshole,' aren't you?"

"No, sir."

"Then, you're dumber than I surmised. That's why you're assigned to the file room." He leaned closer. "I'm really a problem for you, Dotty. A bad nightmare. Every day I will have you in my office to piss you off forcing you to quit. Or. Please make it easy to fire you and deal with the courts to keep you out."

"Yes, sir. Sir?"

"Oh my God. What?"

Dotty stood up. "So, did I win the bet?"

"Get the hell outta my office."

She got the hell out, and found a toothpick.

CHAPTER 5

En route to the file room she bumped into Naim Butler. The University of Pennsylvania Law School intern was rushing and dropped a file he was reading as he walked.

"If your head was up you would've seen me," Dotty said. "You sign that file out? I doubt it, because I'm here."

"I will when I get back." He was gathering papers from the floor. "I think I figured out whose been stealing at Century 21 department store."

"You're still working on thefts at a store with security?"

"Well management believes security is in on the thefts." Naim raised thick, bushy eyebrows eminently crafted for raising. He was in his late twenties and very athletic, with jet black hair and bright brown eyes. "How'd you even know I was looking into the matter?"

"I am in charge of files. I read them. You're wasting your time with the women. Scott Dempsey's your guy."

THE DRUNK DETECTIVE

"So that you know, you're not supposed to be poking your nose in the files. They're confidential."

"What am I supposed to do in that room? Look at porn on my cell phone? I read yours. You ought to take that girl serious."

He blushed. "That isn't your business. Hold up, Queta's not in my personnel record."

"If all your dates were in human resources' data base, you'd be fired. Does Luscious teach you anything?" She smirked.

Naim shifted gears. "So why Scott Dempsey? He's the assistant head of security, why would he steal and risk his job? We've nailed Anita Brockingham ripping off the store five years ago, and she now works for them again."

"Newsflash, we didn't catch a soul. I caught the thieving bitch. It was just before Donna kicked the bucket and left Father Brass Balls to harass me. If you read the files and stop looking for red herrings, you'll learn Dempsey has a side job. Maybe he steals and resells the items on E-bay or in the Amazon store. He could be vying for the head of security job. In order for that to happen the head has to go."

"But how will I find out if he's selling the goods, Dotty? I can't get subpoenas, that you know."

"What the fuck? You're an investigator. Investigate. Tail him. Take photographs. Hack into his laptop from a remote location. I bet he has a broad he's cheating on the wife with in a pink Chanel suit and a new tit job, both of which he paid for, and it won't be Caitlyn Jenner."

"That has nothing to do with the theft. Mr. Goldberg says..."

"Who's case is it? You or his?"

"Mine, but..."

Dotty put her arm around his shoulders. "Listen, clients pay for answers and I assure you he's spending the money on some broad. They all do. Find the girl, get the evidence, and get paid. Clients come back. Goosey Lucy's ecstatic. Your recommendation letter is marvelous. Having integrity is for pussies."

"I guess I can spy on him for a day or two. I have a new car, a Charger."

"That's all the equipment you need to track a person. Trust me, a woman has him risking his job. He'll confess to the thefts to avoid a nasty divorce."

"I hope this works."

"Guts. It's what got me where I am."

"A file clerk."

"Asshole."

"Thanks, though, Dotty. I don't know why Mr. Goldberg wants you run over by an ambulance."

"Screw him. He sleeps with blow up dolls." Dotty went on her merry way to the file room, severely proud of herself. It was like training dolphins at Sea World.

The file room was windowless, a former closet. It was filled with file cabinets, but Luscious had all the files recorded in a computer data base. Dotty was sure Donna Goldberg didn't approve of it, or the fact that Prestige Detective Agency had been using a pen name since her death. Her desk was a legendary Prestige piece with a chair that screamed in pain whenever she sat in it or swiveled in it. On top was the only black rotary phone left in America. First thing, she checked the

THE DRUNK DETECTIVE

wastebasket and found that her pint of Southern Comfort whiskey had been impounded. She took a swig of Wild Irish Rose bum wine from her pocket flask. She mixed her drink colors religiously, not doing so was for punks. Dotty was the youngest of two children of a school janitor and school secretary in rural West Chester, Pennsylvania. The secretary skipped town and took all of the savings and a younger man with her. Dotty's father hated his children afterward and beat them with the Bible as often as he could.

Daily.

Whatever her and her brother did wrong, it was fixed with advice that always began with, 'The Bible says...' Dotty couldn't do anything right, and as soon as she turned seventeen she moved out of her father's house taking her a nice memento: her father's prosthetic leg. He had lost the original one God gave him in a work related accident. In Dotty's mind, he couldn't chase after her with Bible in hand without a leg to stand on. He had her arrested and the judge forced them to therapy. Dotty went to one session alone, because her father refused to participate. She too was banned after she left with the psychiatrist's Smith-Corona electric typewriter on her way out. For this she was arrested a second time in a month, and all hope was lost.

Dotty, however, didn't imagine a fierce crime spree in her future as she wanted no parts of jail. Going to jail was a lovely deterrent for the wild teen. Her intimate knowledge of how criminals worked though gave her the foresight to become a private detective, since no police agency would hire her for her past thefts. She looked through the Yellow Pages for a detective agency that handled divorces. Her parents had been through one, and she knew how to spot the signs of a divorce lurking. Using her brand new typewriter she forged letters from three detective agencies from Miami for one reason only, they were really busy and she doubted they'd be available to confirm her employment especially since she left phony telephone numbers. Donna had hired her on the spot. When a cop Dotty was investigating for his wife figured out that she was eighteen and a high school drop out, Donna Goldberg didn't fire her. She gave her a raise. Besides, the cop's wife paid a handsome boon for the goods to settle her divorce in her favor.

Over Thanksgiving dinner Dotty's father wasn't impressed with her new job. Although, he had forgiven her for stealing the leg, he called her names and guessed that she'd fail, pissing off her big brother, Donald. Donald was carving the turkey when an argument kicked up and he started carving the old man instead, killing him and lowering Black and Decker cordless electric knife stocks. He was found guilty by reason of insanity and currently at Norristown State Hospital for the criminally insane. Dotty told people he was on death row because it sounded more dangerous and he'd likely die there. With dad dead and her brother in jail, Dotty set to move back home, but her mother reappeared and now wanted to claim the house for her and lover boy. Dotty told her to shove the house up her ass and left after she flushed her mother's dentures down the toilet. To Dotty there was nothing more exciting than divorce.

When the flask was dry, she stopped reminiscing, got off her ass, and started filing. There was a short stack of folders on her desk and she peeked in them before placing them in file cabinets. She knew Luscious had all of the good files with the things that were of interest to her locked in his office. Until noon, she went out of her mind in the lonely room and drew faces on pictures of Luscious in the desktop advertising calendar given to clients. Then she went to lunch.

THE DRUNK DETECTIVE

Her favorite bar was Moriarty's Restaurant and Irish Pub on 11th and Walnut Streets, and that was where she was headed. Despite the rain drizzling down she didn't mind the walk. Harry's Bar was closer inside of the Marriott Residence Inn hotel, but she owed, Tommy, the bartender there. Moriarity's had great food and a cheap lunch bar menu for the downtown suits that like to get loose on their lunch breaks like Dotty.

"Hey, Dotty, how you doin'? The usual?" Bebo, the one-eye bandit, black, bartender who owned the place and only worked the lunch crowd with his pit-bull, Puffy. It was at this time he met the investors in his business. This one and the low-key numbers racket he had going on with the South Philadelphia Irishman named, Two Roses Rob, supposedly half Italian and named for the two roses that he left at his three alleged murder scenes.

"Make it a double." Dotty climbed into a stool. The pit-bull, popped his head up from the hardwood floor behind the bar, spied Dotty, yawned and went back to sleep.

Dotty fanned away the stench from Puffy's yawn as Bebo dropped a shot of Seagram's gin and a glass of Corona in front of her. "You need to put mints in the dog's food."

"I gotta stop letting him drink milk."

Dotty demolished the shot and chased it with a gulp of beer. "Hit me, Bebo."

"I can't believe you're here after last night. I was sure you was going to crash that Mercedes." He refilled the shot glass with a little extra.

"Was I here?"

"You don't remember. You danced on the bar. Security had to force you to get down. You then gave a lap dance to Two Roses Rob. That had to be scary."

Dotty looked over her shoulder at Two Roses Rob who was doing a Sudoku puzzle. "Did I make a bet with him."

"What bet?"

She turned back. "You see me make a call?"

"I don't know how you could."

"Did I leave around midnight?"

"Dotty, you came after midnight."

"Do you know where I was before?"

Bebo shook his head. "You're the detective asking me all of the questions."

"This is crazy."

"Must be some shit to lose the whole night."

"I lost all of this year." She knocked back the drink and chased it. "Hit me, again."

"You missed Obama's first inauguration, too, I bet."

Dotty watched him pour. "How'd you lose your eye, anyway?"

"Dick was hard and I looked down to quick," he said as the bar's phone rang. He answered it. With a hand over the mouthpiece: "You here to meet a date named, Rodriguez?"

Dotty took the phone. "Are you following me?"

"Should I be. You are on my list. Your boss gave me a list of places to find you. All bars." The connection smelled of fire. "Can you come by the Round House?"

"As in police headquarters?"

"Yes, I have questions and concerns."

"Like?"

"Like who was out to kill Frankie Robinson. Who would try to fry him? This is definitely arson now. I need you here now, or you may be talking to someone else, and maybe at your job, a fact that I doubt you can stand after talking to your boss."

"Someone else?"

"Homicide, if he dies."

Dotty said she'd be there and hung up. "Fuck me."

"I didn't literally mean my dick poked my eye out. I mean, I'm huge, but you know."

"I got bad news, Dumb-bo."

"Oh, good. You couldn't handle a Viagra induced thirteen-inch schlong."

"Goodbye, Bebo. I have to go." She stood up.

"Payment."

"Today is on you for enduring your bad sex jokes."

Puffy, the pit-bull yawned again.

Bebo waved the fumes with the bar rag. "You got that, Dotty. Tomorrow he'll be on Altoids."

CHAPTER 6

"Let me guess, now you're Miss Marple?"

Rodriguez burped and then offered Dotty a seat. His desk was make of oak with burn marks on the ends closes to him. On his desk was a poorly made Improvised Explosive Device (also known as a booby trap).

"Your kid's science fair project? And stop comparing me to fake TV detectives. These breasts are real, baby."

"No it's an explosive device used to rig the electrical socket. This is a model of the one used in your building. You know how to work it? I doubt it. By the looks of your saggy breasts you haven't worked out in ages."

"By golly, gosh darn it, heavens no, Mr. Fireman. How do you use this thing?"

"You're an ass. Basically, it's used to cross up the wires to create a spark of fire when the switch is turned on. The fire in combination with the fumes from the stove caused the explosion. Quite amateurish, although, painfully effective."

THE DRUNK DETECTIVE

"Now you're cooking with fire," Dotty said with interest and he frowned. "Sorry, bad fire joke."

"Really, though? You're smarter than you...well, than I thought. Any who, we asked your landlord about it and he said every apartment has a light switch at the door. He said that he had all of the electrical wiring replaced less than a year ago. Either he's lying or he was stiffed by an electrician."

"Either is possible knowing Chen. He's a slumlord."

"How cute the way you describe the man that gives you a roof over your head despite your constant late rent payments."

"He told you that? Sounds libelous."

"But yeah. Just before your pal comes home, someone turned on all of the burners on the stove and blew out the flames. The dudes out for the night which is what he does for a living. By the time he gets home the fumes have permeated the place really good. He opens the door, flips the light switch." He banged his hand on the desk. "Boom."

"Jesus." Dotty jumped.

"Because he only weighed one-hundred-fifty-five pounds, he was thrown across the hall instead of being blown to smithereens. The light weight saved his life. The report of the burn unit ain't good. He's burned over fifty-percent of his body."

"I guess his career is over."

Rodriguez didn't say anything. He put a cigarette out on one of the corners of his desk.

"Why'd you want me here. I don't even know how to change the light on my bedroom lamp."

"Yeah. I wanted to ask you what kind of landlord is Chen?"

"He's a real slime-ball."

"You don't like him it sounds like."

"I didn't say that. If I hated slime-balls I'd have no friends."

"You're friends?"

"Look. I didn't say that either."

Rodriguez flipped the butt into a plastic wastebasket and Dotty panicked. She leaned over and saw the bottom of the can filled with water. "I asked about him because he was agitated when I asked had anyone been in the apartment that morning besides Frankie Robinson."

"And he said?"

"He didn't have a clue. Asked if I thought he was a weirdo that peeped out of his door's peephole at his tenants?"

"Did you tell him you did?"

"He's a lying sack of shit. You know liars in this business, he seemed to be protecting someone."

"Man, he wouldn't protect Pope Francis. You badger him like you're doing me?"

"I pushed him to the point that I wanted to take him for a ride in the squad car to a dark area on Delaware Avenue and dump him in the river. See if he could swim. I only called you here because every tenant said you've been living there before they moved in. I assumed you'd know Chen well."

"He takes my coins monthly. That's the extent of it."

"What about the two gentlemen you were with this morning?"

Dotty reached for a toothpick to mask the fact that she had flinched. So Rodriguez was that kind of arson investigator. "I guess you've talked to Lombardo?"

"Should we?"

Holy shit. She didn't know if the old bat or the cop that drilled her gave up the tapes. "I went overboard with the drinks last night," she said. "Maybe I brought two guys back with me for a menage trois. I sent them home around five."

"You're lying through your teeth. Names?"

She huffed. "You ever been white girl wasted? I mean, shit-faced."

"I've drank like a fish, but I smoke mostly."

"The whole bar knows your name, and you theirs. But you don't remember them."

"Where were you drinking?"

"Moriarty's where you called me, for some time. I don't recall before or after that."

"Then you've got a big problem."

"I do. I'm an alcoholic."

"You can't account for everything. No one knows when Frankie went out. Perhaps you and your two pals rigged the booby trap and the gas before the explosion."

"No motive."

"This isn't damn TV, Dotty. I can arrest you without motive and let a prosecutor make that part up."

"But..."

"A hooker, although, a male hooker, could find many easy ways to die. Maybe you had a tab with him." Dotty laughed. "I called another bar looking for you, and learned you hadn't been there since you had a tab." Rodriguez leaned his head to the side and squeezed his eyebrows together. "Bottom-line, if I was you I'd produce those friends."

"What makes me the fall, gal?"

"First of all, you should've told me that two strangers were in the building. Maybe they tricked you to get into the apartment. Your neighbor was blown up that's worth mentioning."

"I didn't see a connection. I walked them out and locked up. What's another?"

"I don't like you at all."

"Trust me, the feeling is soooooo mutual."

"I could give two fucks, Dotty Davis." Rodriguez lit another cigarette. "So you know, it was Mrs. Lombardo that told us thee of you were on the stairs. In between stories about her rendezvous at Sugar House Casino."

"Maybe you should gamble there, but not with me 'cause I didn't try to kill the man. May I go?"

"I have a Mass to get to anyway. Let me know if you plan to leave town. You know the drill."

Dotty stood. "What kind of Mass takes place on Monday?"

"It's a memorial service. The nun, Sister Tudor, principal of my daughter's school died sometime last night. They found her this morning at the pew unresponsive. She was announced dead. You don't look good. You OK?"

Dotty coughed and shot the toothpick right into the wastebasket with the wet butts. "Fine. I almost swallowed that. What did you say the Sister's name was again?"

"Sister Anne Tudor."

"She was my daughter's teacher many moons ago. And to think we had nothing in common. Sure you're OK?"

"I may go back to smoking again, you make it seem so palatable." She left out.

* * *

THE DRUNK DETECTIVE

"Dotty come with me. New rule. I know you love them," said Luscious Goldberg. "No more two-hour lunches."

Jack had sent her right into the office with one of his classic grins. Dotty said, "I had to see a man about a fire."

"You really should watch your words."

"Man?"

"Fire. F. I. R. E. Fire." He sounded like a Spelling Bee contestant.

She stopped at Jack's desk. He was still reading the same paper. What an idiot, she thought.

"Naim Butler around?"

"He left a while ago with a camera around his neck. Luscious gave you hell, huh? Tell me all of the details." He closed the newspaper, leaned back in his chair and cupped his hands behind his head.

"I hope he has a good flash. A young black man with a criminal history looking to be a private investigator. He reminds me of myself."

"You're an old bag. And white. Hardly a good comparison. Besides, he's a vibrant ivy-league law student that was recruited to a firm in New York. They're paying for his law school. He's nothing like you."

"You can hate on me, I'm still the same old G."

"Rapping doesn't make you like him. Oh, this came for you by courier." He held up an envelope.

Dotty didn't take it. "Any windows?"

"Nope."

"My ex-husband's penmanship? I hope ex."

"How the hell I know?"

"Jackie Ottaman serves subpoenas in plain clothes, but she's a county sheriff. Was she a big rectangular gal with a dumb face?"

"You're a big rectangular gal with a dumb face."

She took it. The envelope was heavy cream stock, addressed in fine calligraphy. "'Ms. Dorothy Davis,'" she read aloud.

"Obviously, they don't know you."

She opened it.

{Dear Ms. Davis,

If I am not intruding on prior plans, your presence this evening at six o'clock with be advantageous for you and I.

Very truly yours,

Bernard Sinclair

Papal Nuncio}

A card with a Society Hill address engraved on it was paper-clipped to the letter, along with a new Ben Franklin bill.

"FBI, I hope?" Jack inquired.

"Religious mail." She refolded everything and stuffed it all into in her pocket.

He opened his newspaper. "It's a bit late for that."

CHAPTER 7

"Get lost."

"You shouldn't talk to your partner in crime like that," Dotty said.

"Ex-partner. I got the boot, not you, because of a clause in a will. Now, I'm booting you. Get lost."

Patrick Swayze worked at a Wells Fargo as an assistant manager in Two Penn Center. He had a chiseled face, small frame and dominate black eyebrows like former president Lincoln, which he tried to soften with pastel shirts and Windsor knots in his ties. It was five o'clock on the dot and he was stuffing his briefcase to get out of the office.

"You have a fine job. The boot didn't hurt you one bit," Dotty said.

"You're right. Just my wife and daughter and the freedom I had as a detective. Now I'm in the rat race with these people. I hate you."

"Come on, Swayze."

THE DRUNK DETECTIVE

"Get lost, Dotty."

"Hell it was a sweet case. All you had to do was like I told you and sell the photos to the husband. You weren't supposed to tell Luscious a thing."

"You could've taken the fall since you couldn't be fired. They wanted to have me arrested."

"Well they didn't so what's the problem?" They were walking out of the bank.

Outside, in front of the Clothes Pin Statute, Swayze said, "I was out of work for a year because no one believed I was named Patrick-Fucking-Swayze. Can you imagine that on a resume, if you're not the Dirty Dancing star. My wife divorced me and took my little girl to Florida. I haven't seen either of them in years."

Dotty leaned an elbow on the wall of which on the other side had a twelve feet drop leading to the subway. "Kids cost to damn much, and they turn out to be problems in their teens. Be glad that you're free. I am."

When she came to, she was on her back on the ground being ignored by passerby. Swayze now leaned on the wall and kissed his knuckles.

"What brought you here, Dotty?"

"You've been in the gym, I see." She sat up, tasting blood. "You didn't used to hit me that way. I owe you."

"You weren't as fat and slow either. Get the hell up to, but know I'll knock you back down."

"I believe I have crosshairs on my back."

"I will send the assassin a bonus check."

"I'm not joking."

"Neither am I. There's plenty of money in that bank."

"You hear about the male prostitute that was blown up this morning?"

"Gas explosion? I have."

"Welp, it wasn't an accident."

"OMG, you blew up a man-whore?"

"No, what the hell do I look like?"

"I don't know, but you looked like a pile of dog shit on the ground a second ago."

"It happened in my building. Someone broke in, messed with the light switch, and filled the place with gas before heading out."

"Smart. What was he into besides giving someone's wife pleasure and why're you involved?"

"He was giving more than wives pleasure and obviously pain." Dotty told him the story, beginning with Frankie Robinson's call and finishing with the arson investigator's discovery. She left out the small detail about the staged photos she had created.

"You mean the Sister Tudor the news reported being found by the alter boy at the pew counting Hail Mary's at the Our Lady of the Rosary church this morning?" Swayze asked.

"Thanks to me and a creep, Lynch."

"Tell me more."

"The explosion was for the doll, ain't that the obvious? Lynch thought we were in my apartment and tried to off me and clean up any evidence to link the Church to yet another sex scandal. Luckily, I went back to my place and to bed."

THE DRUNK DETECTIVE

"Missing something. The bishop doesn't need to kill you. He's quite capable of handling scandals."

Dotty sucked her lip to stop the bleeding. "You're a damn fool. This diocese can't take another incident. He'd do anything to keep this quiet, even try to kill me."

"Then you should feel fortunate. Justice missed you by a hair. You've wronged more than ten prostitutes ever could and needed to pay up."

"Screw you. The thing is, I was summoned to the rectory to see the bishop in an hour. Maybe he has a bullet with Dotty written on it."

"Don't go."

"I have to. Could be a business deal."

"You're going to scam the Church. You must have pictures. You're going straight to hell, do not pass GO."

"Just thirty of them. I even took pics of Lynch and his car with the dead nun in the front seat before they pulled off. Oh, and I recorded the pull off until the Caddy turned the corner. They have money, why shouldn't I get some."

"Ask Frankie. He got some money, now look at him."

"I will, but for now I E-mailed you photos to a Dropbox account, but you can't access them unless I am dead. Young kid, Naim Butler, at the agency is going to give you the info if I don't contact you by ten p.m. Here's his number." She handed him a slip of paper with a number written on it.

"I'm not doing that. Fuck you, Dotty."

"Come on, Swayze. I figured your heart was as big as your ass."

He pushed her down. She bounced back up.

"You're pretty strong."

"Been working out. I told you that."

"Look you're the only friend I've got."

"To hell I am. I'm not your friend."

"Come on. I'll call you by ten from my home phone only. Thank God they killed the fire before it hit my place."

"You're one lucky whore. Gin flames aren't easy to put out."

Dotty left, blotting her lip with a handkerchief. She drove towards the rectory with one hand on the steering wheel and the other trying to stop the bleeding, but she could tell it was beginning to swell. She took Market Street right down passing the Gallery Mall and the United States Courthouse. The Society Hill neighborhood was at the end of Market Street (an eight minute drive from the bank), and the Church was right on Fifth and Chestnut Streets, adjacent to the first US Capital.

Her lip stopped bleeding. Before someone answered the door she looked at her face in a compact mirror and stuffed the handkerchief in her pocket.

"Dotty Davis."

Perched in the opened doorway, Lynch looked even more sinister than he did this morning at Frankie Robinson's apartment. He had on the same coat buttoned to the top and his bald head and a little stubble on it in the light.

Dotty's eyes had widened. "I wasn't expecting to see you."

"My Lord is expecting you."

"People know my whereabouts."

"Good for them. Or not." He stepped aside.

Dotty entered the foyer hung with raspberry-colored drapes and followed Lynch down a marble lined hall that looked fresh. At the end Lynch knocked on a door, and a voice invited them inside.

The bishop was a midget of a man with a pouch above his waist mirroring a basketball, with jet-black hair parted in the middle and brushed to each side falling to the white shackle of his clerical collar. He rose from behind a cherry-wood desk, wearing a black cassock that swept the floor and he looked like a wizard in a Harry Potter production on the Avenue of the Arts. The cavernous room was square and smelled of the cheap leather that bound the books on the shelves. A large crucifix made of pearl hung on the wall behind the desk. Lynch and Dotty walked in and the bishop closed the door behind them.

"Thanks for joining us, Ms. Davis," said the bishop. "Take a seat."

"It was the money." She settled into a leather chair that gripped her ass like a hand in a soft glove.

"Were you in an accident?"

"Just my lip."

The bishop took a seat at the desk with his back to the crucifix.

"I wanted to thank you in person for doing such a fine job this morning," he said. "The Church doesn't have to many friends right now. Do you happen to be Catholic?"

"Nope. Too much kneeling. Same reason I couldn't keep my husband."

The bishop nodded as if he understood. "I am quite disturbed by Sister Tudor's indiscretion. I hoped she would be canonized soon and help revive the diocese."

"I guess she found other ways to be revived herself."

He smiled. "I am destined for cardinal. His Holiness practically gave me the red hat during his visit here last year for the Meeting of the Families Celebration. Of course, it's not official, yet."

"You've made plane reservations to Rome and all I bet."

"Don't interrupt His Eminence."

"It's OK, Lynch. If I lost my patience I wouldn't be in this position."

Dotty said, "Your leading lady checking in and then out in a prostitutes bed wouldn't work so good for your image in Rome, I'm sure. Of course, that's why you tried to blow me into tiny pieces."

"How so?"

"The lynch mob director here didn't know that I lived above Frankie. He rigged his apartment to blow my pretty face off, only it blew off Frankie's work equipment."

"What is she talking about?"

"The gigolo's apartment caught fire this morning," Lynch said. "I saw it on the news, that's how I know about it."

"You weren't responsible?"

"Oh my God," Dotty said. "Pardon my French, Father."

"That building is a death trap, Your Excellency. A fire could have easily started there."

THE DRUNK DETECTIVE

"Cops found an IED that started it." Dotty folded her arms, causing the leather to fart. "I have pictures. Lots of them. They're with a friend as we speak. You know the drill."

"You looking to extort the Church?"

"I'm not dressed to be an extortionist. Let's just call it blackmail."

On a serving cart was a silver tray containing two long-stemmed glasses and a cut-crystal decanter half-filled with crimson-colored liquid. The bishop removed the stopper and poured a glass for Dotty and himself.

"We should drink. This post allows me two vices: a little red wine and I smoke a Cuban cigar a day."

"And what are we celebrating, Your Excellency?"

Dotty resisted the urge to touch either glass.

"Your new job as chief of diocesan security. The pay is as handsome as you and the hours are easy."

Dotty smiled and rubbed her hands together. "Am I now Lynch's boss?"

"Dotty please with the dumb questions," said Lynch.

"Lynch works directly for me. The chief of security works without supervision and has an office downtown at the diocese headquarters."

"And in return I develop a case of amnesia?"

"And pass along all relevant material to me, naturally." The bishop sipped from his glass.

Dotty lifted hers then. "What's to stop Lynch from polishing me off after that?"

"Neither Lynch or I had anything to do with that fire. You have a dim view of religion."

"Come on. People getting burned at the stake and nailed to the cross, what'd you expect." She gulped down half her wine. It wasn't that good.

"Are you familiar with the bible, Davis?"

"I knew my dad's up, close and personal. He beat me with it."

"Then you know how important your secrecy is. Do you accept the position?"

"I don't really want to be cooped up in an office. I like my current job. Tell you what: put me on retainer, for a few grand per month to do discreet inquirers, and I keep the pictures for a lifetime. Think of it as a lifetime appointment."

"Not a chance. The pictures are apart of the deal no matter how you slice it."

"Well, you're shit out of luck. 'Scuse my Flen--French." The room was beginning to close and the air thickened. She could barely take a deep breath.

"Your Excellency?"

"Do nothing yet, Lynch."

Dotty's grin spilled all over her face. She dumped the balance of her wine chasing the intoxicating feeling that it gave her. "Don't feel bad Lynch. I know you're not the first person the bishop ordered around." Her vision was blurring and she began to think there was a point to the theory about not mixing the grape with the grain.

"Are you all right, Davis? I fear my company is putting you to sleep."

Dotty could no longer see the bishop or the crucifix behind him. They were both shadows. She leaned over to return her glass to the tray and kept going, to the floor.

THE DRUNK DETECTIVE

She thought, dammit, I bet this means no job either.

CHAPTER 8

She awoke feeling no different than she did every other morning, with her head pounding and a tongue blown up the size of a Boeing seven-forty-seven. Her eyes were glued shut with crust.

She rubbed them, pried them open, and thought she had lost her sight. A street lamp beamed on her and she shifted forcing a cheap bottle of wine to fall to the floor of the judge's luxury car. Something in three jackets and a man's fedora was on the floor prying off her shoes.

"What are you doing?"

A dirty face looked up at her. An old fashioned face, possibly female, slim nostrils, blood shot eyes, and no more than two teeth in a pink hole of a mouth. Dotty smelled wine. Or maybe whiskey.

"I assumed you were here because you were dead," said the monster.

"I'm not."

THE DRUNK DETECTIVE

"Are you certain? I seen dead rats get up and scurry away because no one told them."

"Retard. Get off my damn feet."

"Dead people don't need shoes. I don't know why people waste money burying dead people in them."

"Old man, you don't either."

He moved back. "You're parked in a cemetary. No need to be here if you're alive."

"What?" Dotty popped up and looked around at all of the headstones.

"Yes. Greenmount Cemetary."

"Jesus. You sure this ain't the Marriot Hotel."

He cackled. It sounded like ice being chopped in a blender. "Now that I think about, maybe it is. This here is a Philadelphia cheese steak. Sorry no fries." He pulled a dead mouse from a jacket and dangled it by its tail.

"You eat mice?"

"You can have half for the shoes."

{Where's my gun,} Dotty thought. {Maybe the glove box.} She popped it open and the man threw his hand up and caught a fifth of vodka. He unscrewed the cap and took a huge swig. Dotty reached for the other bottle and took a long pull. As she let the liquor warm her belly, she pondered about Patrick Swayze. He was supposed to call the cops at ten.

"Give me my lucky ascot asshole."

"I didn't take no ascot. Do I look like I wear fuckin' ascots?"

She turned on the car and looked at the clock. It was 10:16. "Holy macro."

"I have to go."

"Leave me the rest of the bottle."

"Get lost." She slammed the door shut and swung the car out onto Front Street. She drove through the Hunting Park section of North Philadelphia hoping not to be carjacked in the crime ridden area. The area was home to turf wars, prostitution, and the drug trade. Even Lynch treaded lightly after dropping her off so far from downtown.

Her time with the bishop was still a blur. Whatever the bishop had slipped her had to have been clear and in her glass before he handed it to her. Surely a premeditated attempt to show her who was in charge. Why didn't he just kill her? Certainly, Lynch could handle that. Whatever the drug was it was good, because her memory was back and she even knew where she was the night before. As luck would have it, she had had a marvelous night.

She got onto the busy, and heavy populated Broad Street, and called Swayze from her cell phone.

"Hello?"

"Patrick. Dotty."

"Get out of my life."

"Stop the jokes, OK. Did you send the photos to the cops, yet?"

"Huh? Photos? What are you talking about?"

"The ones I E-mailed for you, idiot."

"Oh, no, I didn't."

"You're an ass. Why not?"

"Why not what?"

"If you didn't hear from me you was supposed to send them off."

"OK, I didn't. Move on."

"What's the point in using you if you're not going to do your part?"

"You're right. Did you pay me? Did you get any money out of the Church?"

"I got drugged."

"What's new?"

"Man, they slipped me something. Knocked me out and I awoke in a cemetary with a bum trying to take my penny loafers."

"Only a bum would want them."

"Look, Swayze, if you don't hear from me in twenty-four hours, please get the pics to a cop named, Rodriguez. He's an arson investigator."

"OK, when do I get my money?"

"Listen, if you have to send the pics I'll be dead."

"Then I'll be a winner." He hung up.

Dotty hung up and imagined being confronted by Chen as soon as she walked into the apartment building about his cut of {her} money. Her landlord wanted money. Her pal, Patrick, also wanted money. Neither of them realized, she wanted to squeeze money out of someone just as bad. The money from the he-bitch was chump change and Chen had already put a dent in it. She hoped Chen hadn't reported her little tampering with a crime scene to the police. She dialed the massage parlor and Chen's home number and both rang nine-thousand times without an answer.

Chen had never went anywhere. He had his groceries delivered and was a frequent online shopper. Where the hell could he be?

"The precinct. Dammit." Dotty hurried around a SEPTA bus and spun the Benz's wheels just over sixty mph.

Chen didn't own a car and hated to pay for taxis. He surmised he'd be kidnapped by an UBER driver and thought it was the riskiest business created since prostitution. Dotty made a left onto Vine Street and hoped she'd intercept Chen walking to the cop house. She knew his distinct walk and knew she'd see it a mile away. Dotty thought she saw him posted up at a corner, but it turned out to be an inflatable doll that some idiot had leaned on one of the last phone booths left in the city.

The massage parlor was pitched black, with the CLOSED sign in the window over Kim Kardasian's boobs. Dotty paralleled into the space where Lynch's vehicle had been earlier and slid into the apartment's foyer. The security buzzer hadn't worked since Clinton's first term.

Dotty knocked on Chen's door and waited.

"You're probably looking at me through the peephole, you fucker. Open up," she said, knocked again, and then turned the knob.

She walked right on into the apartment. It was neat with the kind of flare made for an apartment in Trump Tower. It was obvious how he spent his money collecting poor people's rent. "Pompous bastard," she said and helped herself to a Mike's Hard Lemonade in a well appointed kitchen.

She walked around swishing the cooler in her mouth to get rid of the poisoned wine taste.

No Chen.

She helped herself to a Swarovski crystal shot glass before heading to the door. She had no idea where Chen was, but it wasn't like him to call or go to the police, period; especially,

THE DRUNK DETECTIVE

when the money came if he didn't. Free money was Chen's first wish if asked by a genie.

Brooding if he might be at Frankie Robinson's place assessing the damage, or creating more, for insurance policy purposes, Dotty hopped off of a mohair sofa, locked up (there were thieves in the building), and bound the stairs to Frankie's apartment. The hallway smelled of smoke and stale water drying.

Chen wasn't there, either. The door to the burnt apartment was boarded by crime scene tape. She doubted that he was in there.

She went up to her floor, hoping Chen hadn't used his key and was waiting in her apartment. The key really was pointless considering Adam the fireman and his chop for gigolos.

Dotty's first thought was that she needed to get her place in order. She needed to throw everything away and start over from scratch. The living room sofa was faux leather which was peeling and missing leather exposing cotton. A travesty. Thanks to the wine, the spiritual wine, her memory was slowly resurfacing. Why was her glove box in such disarray that the vodka bottle popped right out when she opened it? The bum had no reason to leave it there.

Lynch did.

She wondered what had he learned about her from being in there, besides she had liquor, which wasn't so bad since the bishop drank wine and smoked cigars.

Dotty walked towards her bedroom anticipating a shower. The door was shut, something that she never did. {Where's my gun?} Having no idea, she grabbed a small bat kept on her mantle by the front door in case she had to bludgeon a robber to death. She eased open her bedroom door and then barged in. Inside the door she tripped, lost her balance, did a ungraceful pirouette, and slammed onto the bed. Luckily. Finally, God was on her side. She bounced up, flicked on the light, and looked at Chen. Chen was what had tripped her.

The landlord was on his back, spread eagle, and undoubtedly dead. A Versace ascot was wrapped into a Windsor knot around his neck.

"Now, Chen, how'd you get my lucky ascot around your throat?"

CHAPTER 9

"Evening, Mrs. Lombardo," Dotty said.

The dame was in nursing scrubs and a leather bomber. She paused before descending the stairs, found her glasses out of her pocket, and peered through them at Dotty. "I thought that was your stuffy voice. You sound awful." She knew how to throw shade and be totally oblivious to it. "Who's that with you, hun?"

"Just a pal, ma'am." She leaned harder into Chen's soggy frame to stop him from forming a pile of poop on the old runner.

"Looks like Chen to me," she said. "You better get the stench of smoke outta my place, Chen. Don't tilt your head at me, mister China man."

Dotty laughed. She said, "He's a little choked up from smoke inhalation. You know he's as old as you. I'm taking him for a drive to get some fresh air."

"Yeah, yeah. You had him up there drinking, I bet. The whole building knows what you're into, Detective Dotty."

"Don't you have to get to work, ma'am?"

"Pardon me. I know that. I was wiping asses at that nursing home before you were born."

"Point taken. Good night, Mrs. Lombardo."

"Just a tragedy what happened to that young man, Frankie. I mean, he turned a few tricks, but that was no reason to blow him up. Don't look at me like that, Chen. The whole building knows you're a pimp. He tricks and gives you money. You sly, China man."

"Right. Just horrible." Dotty's shoulder was going to sleep and cramping. "Well, good night."

"Did your other friend get home OK earlier?"

"Absolutely. She needed rest and is really resting in peace now."

"Hell, Chen doesn't look much better. You gotta stop drinking with light weights. Apparently, they can't tolerate the white lightening like you."

"I guess, you're right. Good night, Mrs. Lombardo."

"Don't forget the smell of smoke."

"He won't, ma'am."

She moved past them and made her way down. The street door locked behind her, then Dotty lifted Chen as if he was a bride and carried him to the first floor. The landlord weighed as much as a jockey, much less than Sister Tudor. She rushed because she couldn't bump into any other residents of the building. Mrs. Lombardo was a non-factor. No jury would believe her word. Dotty thought about waiting until four a.m. because apparently that was the perfect time to move a dead body. At the rate she was going, she'd have the art of moving corpses down to give a TED talk.

At the bottom, she gently sat Chen on the floor not to cause post-mortem marks. She remembered Lynch's stellar guidance, fishing into Chen's pocket for his keys. She opened the door to his lair, and inside laid Chen on his sofa and grabbed a magazine from a coffee table. She placed the news rag on Chen's chest opened to the infamous page six and crossed his arms on his stomach. With regret, she took the earlier stolen Swarovski thingy from her pocket and put it back in its place. Someone knocked on the door.

"Mr. Lee Chen? Lee Chen?"

Dotty froze like a seasoned cat burglar. The voice calling out for Chen belonged to arson investigator, Rodriguez.

"Are you home, sir? Just a few questions." He knocked some more forcing Dotty to jump. Her nerves were shot, but she remained cool.

She looked for the nearest window and past the body splayed out on the sofa unresponsive. She wanted to set off an IED to blow the door right into Rodriguez to knock him out, so that she could escape. The doorknob began to turn. She couldn't remember if she had locked the door before she put the landlord in the place he'd be found and pronounced dead.

With luck, the knob stopped turning. Someone jiggled it, though. Then there was silence, and Dotty needed Bourbon. Or maybe, vodka. Perhaps another Mikes Hard Lemonade from the landlord. She became nostalgic for the stink breath dog at Moriarty's. She prayed the cop wasn't looking for a spare key or a way to break in.

Then she heard footsteps fading away before they began to climb the stairs.

THE DRUNK DETECTIVE

Dotty waited a second before she tiptoed over to the door and put an eye to the peephole in the door. The foyer was empty. Quickly she opened the door slipped out, and into the vestibule. Rodriguez started back downstairs. She put her cell phone to her ear, and said, "You know I really hate you. I am home now, and I am hanging up before my husband hears me," as she met Rodriguez in the foyer.

The arson investigator had a cigarette dangling from his mouth. "Our neighbors are complaining to Chen about the smell of smoke. Mrs. Lombardo, in fact, you remember her."

Ash leaked onto the floor. "I have some questions for Chen, like what time did Frankie Robinson usually get in. Or do you know?"

"Times varied. He didn't have a traditional 9-5 or set hours of operation from his lovely home-based business, you know?"

"Don't be an ass. That's why I asked."

"Look, I wasn't sleeping with him, so our times didn't have to synchronize."

"That's my issue. Since no one knows his hours, how'd the person that set up the explosion know when it'll be safe to get into the apartment?"

"Tough question, but maybe the perp is a woman and set a fake appointment at a hotel to be sure he wasn't home. Have you checked his credit cards and cell phone records."

"He's not dead, yet, so no. Do you mind if we go to your place to chat some more?"

"Can it be later? I have a date."

"No. I could just go up. Perhaps, you forgot your door was busted through."

"I forgot."

"Another blackout, huh?"

"Nope. Not at all. Just been busy. Work stuff."

"Really. In the file room. Don't look shocked, I know you're a bona fide file clerk. We can chat here. Any idea about who you brought into the building last night?"

"Been working on it. Got a date at the same bar tonight to try to get some answers for you."

"Really. I hope you can get me what I need. Listen, I'm going to let you go to your date to get the answers that I need."

"Perfect. Maybe they need you at HQ. You should get going."

"News to me." Ash fell on his blazer and he didn't bother to brush it off. "He might make it."

"He who?"

"Frankie Robinson. Docs say he's breathing on his own. Third degree burns may kill his career if he comes out of the coma, though."

"That's a good thing. I hope he recovers."

"Me too, or this turns into a murder case. I looked through the hole in your apartment door."

Christ. "OK. Hopefully, you didn't violate my Fourth Amendment right."

"You live in a sty for animals, the explosion or fireman?"

"I can't blame anyone. Just have been busy working on cases and hadn't had time to clean up."

"Oh, OK." He turned and opened the door. He paused. "Hey where's your ascot?"

"Ascot?"

"Yes, the one you had on at my office right around your neck."

"Neck?"

"I was impressed by the ascot. Women like you don't usually wear them."

"Oh." Dotty got her feelings back. "Good night, sir."

"Yup. Good night. And remember, you're still on my list."

When Rodriguez left Dotty went back to her apartment and drowned the last drops from a vodka bottle, before splashing water on her face.

Two scenarios. Either Chen had caught Lynch tearing up her apartment looking for the pictures and got himself choked for it, or it happened when Lynch came in search for it and discovered Chen already in her apartment snooping around. It didn't matter to Dotty. She liked Chen despite their problems about her rent always being late. She'd keep his camera as a memento. She worked the camera to see if it was any good after being smashed, as she dialed Patrick Swayze at his condo.

"Dotty, please, get out of my life."

"The stakes have been raised. The pictures are quite important now."

"You get my cut yet?"

"No. Not yet for crying out loud. I'm checking on my insurance policy. Things are getting out of control."

"That's just your weight."

"C'mon, Swayze."

"Don't get your panties in a snare. The pictures are safe and sound."

"Thanks, best bud."

"I'm not your bud, you ass. I can't get my coins if I don't keep my end of the bargain, dummy." He hung up.

Oddly, Dotty felt like shit. If that was even possible in her life of drunken debauchery. Someone--maybe her--would have major problems when Chen was found dead. Landlords weren't on anyone's Christmas list, especially immigrants that ran massage parlors. The list of suspects ranged from chronic late rent payers (Dotty included), tenants that wanted the smell of smoke removed from the place (Dotty included), and the whole diocese. Which, under close scrutiny, may be right on the money. Mrs. Lombardo had seen Dotty with two dead bodies, but she was no prosecutor's star witness. All Dotty had to do was keep her crimes to herself. She doubted Lynch would rat her out. Or Bishop Sinclair. One fact remained simple: Lynch didn't get the film or photos of his beloved Sister Tudor, so Dotty was a lot more deadly to the Church if she was dead than alive.

Somewhat relieved, Dotty looked through her apartment, and wanted to make a fraudulent claim with FEMA to help get it cleaned up, so that she could find her gun. It was a cute, little Walther PK380 semi-automatic eight shot number that she used once to ward off a crazy husband that chased her after throwing hot beans in his face. It was then he decided she wasn't worth the trouble and he split with their daughter. Out of love for them, Dotty let them both go away and never looked for them. Now with her front door a wreck she wanted the gun close by, especially since her landlord wouldn't be buying a new door. She couldn't find it, however.

Realizing suddenly that she hadn't taken Mrs. Lombardo's advice and was drinking without out eating, she scooted to the refrigerator looking for food that wasn't in the form of liquid. She came up with a half of a cheese steak, popped it into the microwave and then drowned it in cheap squeeze cheese and ketchup before swallowing it. She was amazed at how good a two-day old cheese steak tasted.

Pushing unfolded clean laundry from one side of the sofa to another, she plopped down and decided to catch reruns of Forensic Files, the source for her arsenal of investigative tactics. To her dismay the back of the TV was removed. {You bitch," she thought of Lynch or Chen. Her need for a TV and door made her think of Frankie Robinson. His call was starting to cost her far more than previously thought. She decided to get to bed early, taking her mini-bat with her just in case Lynch returned.

The telephone pulled her out of a dream; she was at Liquor Palace, a hotel that poured liquor out of the faucets instead of water.

"Whoever you are, you'd better hang up right now, or I'll find out where you live and communicate with ISIS from your home computer, calling the FBI from your home phone to report you before I slip out."

"Amazing, you're so chipper." The caller cleared his throat. "Dotty we need to talk."

"Not this time. Who the hell are you?"

"This is Scott Sinclair."

"Who the hell is Scott Sinclair?"

"Bishop Sinclair, Dotty. Tell me you drink so much that you don't recall."

She perked up and looked at her Mickey Mouse watch. {You son of a bitch," she thought. "It's after midnight." She groaned.

"Thank you. It's a fresh new day. New horizons brewing. Can you meet me at Our Lady Of the Rosary rectory at noon."

"And let you slip me another bad batch of the Church's sacred wine?"

"I am deeply sorry about that. If you'll meet me for lunch, I'll show you how much."

"I would never eat or drink in your company. No way, Jose."

"OK, fine. Just meet me, because I accept the terms of your job proposal. We should discuss this in detail over food and wine."

"No food. I'll be there, and I'll be bringing my own bottle of wine."

CHAPTER 10

Our Lady of the Rosary was a compound with a church, rectory, and a K-12 school in Center City's Society Hill area. It covered an entire city block steps away from the Constitution Center and drew visits from sitting US Presidents. Dotty parked, dashed inside the church and was enveloped by a vaulted echoing interior with three sections of pew with navy-blue-colored runners in the aisles between. At the feet of a twelve-foot crucifix with a porcelain Jesus, a teenaged boy dressed in a white robe was busy lighting candles.

"Hey, young man." The words assaulted every wall.

The boy continued to light candles.

"What's your name, pal?"

"Jonathan Gotti."

"Bullshit."

"That's what everyone says. You shouldn't use curse words, and especially not in the Church."

THE DRUNK DETECTIVE

"My apologies. What do I owe five Hail Mary's, Jon Gotti?"

"I don't know."

"Where's your boss?"

Gotti nodded towards Jesus.

"The one one on earth, Bishop Sinclair?"

"I think the rectory."

"OK, thanks. You're awfully good with the lighter. You smoke?"

"No, ma'am."

"Drink?"

"No, ma'am."

"Curse?"

"No, ma'am!"

"Wow, you must live in a home with a single mom. You need an old man."

The boy pointed out a miniature version of the cathedral surrounded by rosebushes. Dotty left Gotti and pushed a button by the rectory's front door. When no one answered on the second buzz, she tried the knob. Maybe the bishop was asleep. She'd love to get photos of him in the buff, for blackmail purposes.

After twenty minutes, Dotty used her cell phone to call Bishop Sinclair. It rang several times.

"This is Bishop Sinclair."

"I'm on the steps, Your Bishopness," Dotty said. "Where the fuck you been the last half hour?"

"...can't come to the phone right now..."

{Bullshit. This is going to be added to the bill mister.} On her way out, she asked Gotti to relay a message, "Tell the bishop that I was here and he can reach me at home."

"OK."

"You seen him today, kid?"

"As a matter of fact, no."

"Interesting. OK. have a nice day."

* * *

During the drive home, Dotty had quite the time seeking puddles with pedestrians standing or walking nearby and ran the fancy car through them. Whenever she splashed one with dirty water, she celebrated with a gulp from her flask. At a bus stop she scored three senior citizens, a FED-EX driver, and a blind man with a seeing eye dog, and drank all of the contents left in the flask. Little awards. If she had quit her job for nothing, she'd send the pictures to the Associated Press and help Bishop Sinclair say goodbye to any ascension with the Church.

Nearing her apartment, Dotty received a call from the arson investigator.

"I need you to meet me over at U of Penn hospital ASAP. Frankie's up and talking about nothing. He refuses to divulge who tried to blow him up to anyone but you."

"I'm not a cop. I can't help him. And I hate lawyers, so, I know none. Unless I need help."

"Well you must have a way with men, because he wants to see you now, and so does his brother."

"Is that right? I do have a way with men." She was looking in her rearview mirror blushing.

"Get your ass over here." He hung up.

THE DRUNK DETECTIVE

Twenty minutes later Dotty walked onto Frankie's hospital room floor and found Rodriguez smoking a cigarette.

"That has to be illegal and unhealthy for patients," she said without preamble.

He flicked ashes onto the floor.

"Fuck you."

"Pardon me?" A mean faced orderly stopped and glared at Dotty.

"Talking to the cop." She stood with her back against the wall. "Why am I here?"

"Because you have many enemies for seventy and this is one."

"I'm fifty-six. Don't push your luck, Hun."

"No shit. Jesus life has been rough on you. All that time in the file room."

"Man, please. You're far from Tom Cruise."

"Back to the point, the man here says fuck you. Why?"

"No idea."

"Where were you last night?"

"Paddy's Old City Pub on Second and Race from happy hour to nine."

"You could've left there and rigged the switch. Where else?"

"Moriarty's Bar from nine-ten until eleven. Some dude pumped me full of drinks."

"I find that hard to believe; you're not pretty enough. Anyone else would remember you? A bartender?"

"Both should. I was pretty shit-faced."

"You're shit faced now and reek of terrible, cheap liquor."

"That's fine. But that's where I was. Why are we doing this in a hospital hallway?"

"Because I want to. What about the two guys Mrs. Lombardo saw you with this morning?"

Dotty suddenly wanted to do the unthinkable: to tell the truth. At this point she was guilty of withholding evidence, the kind of charge that wasn't a big deal. Maybe there was a law about improper disposal of a nun; but she could beat that too. A bishop had ordered her to bring the woman who died naturally home. On the flip side, the fact that Lynch had strangled Chen while tearing up her place convinced her the photos were worth their weight.

"Can't recall," she said.

"I don't get it. Why not?"

"Look, I forgot."

"Problem is yesterday you knew nothing and now you know all of your places and times, but no idea about who you brought home. Your alibis."

"I didn't rig the man's apartment to blow him up. No motive to and I would have messed up my own lovely home."

He chuckled. "You know I believe you. But something is off here."

"That's your job to get it on. So, is Frankie going to awake or what?"

"Yes, but who knows when he will be able to talk."

"You bitch." Dotty buttoned her coat. "I knew he wasn't up asking for me. I'm out of here, if you don't mind."

"I don't, but I'll be looking into these alibis. As…"

THE DRUNK DETECTIVE

"I'm still on your list."

"You got it. Before you go," the arson investigator said, signaling for a tall, handsome man to join them. "Dotty meet Frankie's brother, Hank Robinson."

"You can call me Hankie, ma'am."

She held out her hand and he grabbed it. She did a curtsy, and said, "You are a tall glass of chocolate milk, Hankie Pankie."

"What was that?"

"I digress."

"OK, I'd like to talk to you. Without the arson investigator, I mean."

Dotty had already been eyeing Hank—couldn't help it—as he stood outside of Frankie's hospital room, but right in her line of sight. He was about Dotty's height, lean in a pink Polo Ralph Lauren polo shirt, blue jeans, and Timberland boots. His features were refreshing and smooth like Frankie's, but they had to have one different parent. He looked more like twenty-five than forty-five. They retreated to the end of the hallway and he smiled at her.

"Thanks for saving my brother."

"No problem," she said. "I didn't actually save him from death as I was dead as this floor when the explosion occurred, but I rescued him from something much bigger that he needs to wake up and tell you about."

"That makes sense. He's always been known to get into trouble. I'm the good son. I haven't talked to him since we were little. Our parents gave up on him long ago. They're strict Evangelicals."

"What a shame."

"Our lives went on without him when he filmed himself masterbating and posted it on PornHub, and a member of the church found it and told the whole congregation. Some people watched the vid. When I saw him on the news, though, I was compelled to come here to help him."

"The cop lied and told him that he was conscious, son of a bitch."

"Whoa, ma'am. The language."

"I'm grown."

"A woman shouldn't talk that way." He put a hand on her shoulder and she dithered. "I'm working on a doctorate degree at U Penn, so I'd appreciate if you stayed in touch just in case he awakens. Maybe we can do lunch. I owe you for Frankie."

"Like a date?"

"Probably," he said and smiled. "Whatever floats your boat, ma'am."

"Dotty. You can call me, Dotty."

"Ms. Dotty if I'm nasty."

She covered her mouth and chuckled. "I guess you're not as born again as your parents?"

"I am. Just super flirty. But I have to go. When and if he awakens call me and I will do the same." He handed her business card with a name and number printed on it, but no profession.

"No problemmo," she said. "I am just going to tuck this into my bar, I mean bra. If the police badger your brother to much about what he did be sure he knows that I have pictures to make them back off. He'll understand."

THE DRUNK DETECTIVE

"Oh, I'm sure. You're a detective, I bet you have compromising pics."

"I certainly do. I'll be in touch if I learn anything."

CHAPTER 11

Shortly after two a.m. Dotty staggered into her apartment having drunk away the realization that she never made an anonymous call to have Chen cleaned up. She was sickened, but protecting her own backside trumped the idea of saving his. She sat on her bed and the telephone rang. "Whoever you are, you better be dying?"

"I'm dying to know why you haven't checked in. I was beginning to think you scored cash from the bishop and skipped town."

"Swayze?"

"Who else? So did you get paid?"

"What?"

"The bishop. Jiminy Cricket. Did you make a deal to sell the pictures?"

"Working on that. Treat this like a post-job interview: I'll call you, don't call me." She hung up.

THE DRUNK DETECTIVE

She was stretched on her bed in all of her clothes when her phone rang again.

"Patrick Swayze, Jesus."

"You dreaming of the Dirty Dancing sexy version, or the To Wong Foo Thanks For Everything gay one?" It was Rodriguez.

"I'm mad that you know the entire title." Dotty drew a deep breath. "It's two-thirty a.m."

"Thank you. This the twentieth time I've tried to call both of your numbers and I E-mailed you. I contacted all of the bars you told me about yesterday."

"We gotta talk now?"

"You were truthful, I wouldn't go back to Moriarty's if I were a sane person."

"What's the deal?"

"Homicide, buddy-o-pal. You've left out some details in our prior chats."

Chen. Dotty shot up, moaning with her bones cracking, and groped around for her flask. It wasn't in bed with her. "Shit. Where are you? Downstairs?"

"Hell no. Why would I be there? I'm in Society Hill."

"Society Hill?"

"Society Hill. Is there an echo on the line?"

"What's in Society Hill?"

"Point blank. One dead bishop."

"Bullshit. Sinclair?" She immediately slapped her leg. "Oh, God."

Pause. "You said that faster than a contestant on Family Feud looking to play."

She feverishly looked for her flask. She found it. Drank the one available drop.

"Dotty Davis, you still with me?"

"Yes. I don't know nothing 'bout a dead bishop."

"Funny. You knew his name."

"Lucky guess of a trained dick."

"Well tell me what's next in this case?"

Dotty said nothing.

"Yup, I hear heavy breathing. I need you to meet me..."

"Look, I'm not going to meet you anywhere."

"Meet me at the precinct or I'll have so many police cars on your block to search every apartment including Chen's to fuck with your neighbors. He'll surely kick you out just like your boss did."

"I quit."

"I talked to him, too. He fired you. I can assure you that your day will start quite badly if I have to come there. Two dead clergy from the same parish is looking like one killer. You want to tell me something?"

"Yes. I am not the killer."

"That was something. You own a gun?"

"If you want to call it that. I haven't seen it in weeks." Dotty began to sweat from every pore. Lynch hadn't left her apartment empty-handed after all.

"Rigors in full swing, 'bout six hours. Could be longer. He has powder burns on his face. Killer pressed the gun right to his forehead. We think he knew and expected the murderer."

THE DRUNK DETECTIVE

"I can't hit the LOVE sign in Love Park at point blank range."

"Good, but I'll need you down at the precinct ASAP to run some test on you."

"I'm not in need of any tests. My health is good."

"Your liver is on it's last breath I am sure. Powder burn tests. Prints. Polygraph."

Dotty said, "Oh, that'll clear my name. I'll be there after I report a burglary."

CHAPTER 12

They locked her in a tank with a stiletto murderer, a pair of butch-lesbians accused of extorting and sodimizing a gay club owner, and a farm girl awaiting extradition to Florida to answer charges of conspiracy to commit robbery, home invasion, and breeding horses in a residential zone.

The butch-lesbians minded their own business, and the stiletto killer seemed content laying on the concrete floor rubbing her feet. Her shoes (size 12 Manolo Blahnik pumps) were collected as evidence in a murder. The farm girl befriended Dotty. She ran north of three hundred pounds and close to six-feet-four inches with hair down to her ass, Dotty was not inclined to ignore her. Her name was Alexiah.

"Dotty," she said laying an arm on Dotty's shoulder's forcing her to sag, "you like horses?"

"Not particularly. You can't eat them."

"Click. Clack," said the stiletto murderer.

"You see that bitch face when I punched his ass?" asked one of the butch-lesbians.

"You'd be surprised all of the uses of horses," said Alexiah, pulling Dotty closer to her. "Do you like horses now?"

"Well give me an example?" Dotty's reply was choked.

"Click. Click. Clack," said the stiletto murderer.

"That wasn't nothing compared to when you stuck the pipe up his ass," said the other butch-lesbian.

"Anyway, horses isn't all we got in Florida. We got oranges," Alexiah said. "They give oranges with everything. Ever have orange juice and a plate of orange slices with breakfast?"

"No. That's odd."

"Click. Clack. Click. Clack," said the stiletto murderer.

"We shouldn't have left it up his ass. Your prints may be on it," said the first butch-lesbian. "You twirled that pipe around and round, gaping his hole. He probably loved it."

"What you locked up for, Dotty?" asked Alexiah.

"They say I killed two bishops."

"You're going to hell. Two? Yeah, you're done. God hates you. The whole Catholic diocese will be outside the courthouse when you go for bail."

"Tell me something that I don't know."

"You should get a horse. They never die on you. When they do you can eat them despite what people say."

"Click. Click. Click. Click. Clack!" said the stiletto murderer.

Alexiah was telling Dotty about a sexual escapade with a horse when the turn-key officer came. "Davis."

"Present." Dotty raised her hand.

The cop shook his set of keys and inserted one in the lock. "Let's go. You're out. Your lawyer's here."

"What's his name? I called three in honor of the trinity."

"The deaf one in an orange suit. Looks like a clown. He's been here over the years."

"Oh, Doc Brennan."

"Hey," said one of the butch-lesbians, as the cop was re-locking the bars behind Dotty. "When do we eat?"

"Soon."

"Better be. We need something down the pipeline sooner than later." The other butch-lesbian chuckled.

"Take care of yourself, Dotty," said Alexiah, through the bars. "Don't forget me."

"I seriously doubt it, honey."

Larry Brennan was waiting in the discharge room, along with Sergeant Rodriguez, Lieutenant Boxer, and, behind the desk, another Philadelphia PD officer who had processed Dotty three hours earlier. The officer emptied a manila envelop full of Dotty's valuables onto a wood counter engraved with many other releasees street monikers and checked them off against a list on a clipboard.

"One silver flask."

"Hello, Dotty." Brennan took Dotty's hand in his wet palm. He was a short, Irish man in his seventies, with manicured nails and a hearing aid. He was often mistaken for a fancy dressed private doctor thanks to all of his loud suits.

"What's up, doc? How's Barb?"

"One plastic toothpick holder."

THE DRUNK DETECTIVE

"It's been a while, Dotty. Barb's two wives back. It's Amazing Amy now."

"Oh. Wasn't you married to Francine, too?"

"No, you're thinking Francesca. This one's a cheerleader."

"Wow. Temple U."

"Northeast High. She's barely legal."

"I thought you seemed weak."

"Viagra script only helps so much."

"One pork-bound notebook."

"It's called pig skin. What happened to the other two lawyers that I called."

"Jared Johnson's wanted for child support payments and ducking any new cases just in case the ex-wife proves paternity. Robert Roberts is in intensive care at Einstein Med Center. He forgot to show up for rapper Meek Mills' probation violation hearing last week. Someone reminded him to never miss another court appearance."

"One gold pinky ring."

"Well I'm elated to see you, Doc. Thanks for getting me released."

"One silver pinky ring."

"The sarge and the LT here were scared of my presence so they dropped the absurd accusations."

"One pinky ring, perhaps white gold."

Dotty looked at Rodriguez and Boxer, smiled. Rodriguez grinned and dropped a cigarette butt on the tiled floor. "It's LT Boxer's case."

"One female condom."

"The ME put Sinclair's death at approximately eleven a.m. and two," Boxer said, adjusting a boring clip-on tie. "You were with Luscious Goldberg at eleven-thirty, being fired."

"I quit," she said. "For the record."

"An altar boy at Our Lady of the Rosary says you were at the cathedral before noon and stayed about an hour and a half. Soon after you met my sergeant at the hospital. It's hardly possible a woman of your caliber pulled off a murder with these strict times recorded by trust worthy people."

"I resent that. I'm quite capable, but..."

"I doubt it. You couldn't have been fi..."

"Quit my job."

"With Goldberg and made a perfect route to kill the bishop. That would've required no traffic and all green lights in Center City. I can't hold you."

"One multi-color ascot, Versace," said the police officer behind the desk.

"Well, I gotta go folks."

"Two matchbooks from Dave and Busters and Delilah's Strip Club."

"Before you go, can you be a Barbie doll and tell me about your business with Bishop Sinclair."

"Thirteen .380 slugs, two Canadian pennies, and a Susan B. Anthony dollar piece. Sign on this line."

Dotty signed the receipt and stuffed her belongings into her pockets. "I wanted to give my condolences to the good nun punching her ticket to the Upper Room."

Brennan took off his fedora, ran a finger over his bald head.

THE DRUNK DETECTIVE

"Come on, Dotty, the bishop was killed with your gun."

"And it was stolen from my place."

"Speak up, Dotty."

Dotty gave a wicked glare at her attorney. "I thought this is when you tell me to shut the hell up."

"My batteries died." Brennan removed the hearing aid and smacked it into his palm.

Rodriguez stomped his foot at a new burn mark on his necktie. "I guess this is the end of the road for us, Dotty. Too bad Frankie survived. The case has been assigned to Lieutenant Boxer."

"Tell me he's alive."

Lt. Boxer said, "We do attempt homicides, too. And I know about a fact that you know: there's a connection between who tried to blow up Frankie and who did shoot Bishop Sinclair. You may not tell me today, but I'm coming for you because I know you know that connection."

"I have Sprint, very bad service. I know nothing about good connections. I see you're clairvoyant, though."

"That's fine. You'll get an upgrade."

"Fuck you, Lieutenant."

"Speak up, Dotty," Brennan said.

Dotty snatched the hearing aid out of the lawyer's hand, put it to her lips, and shouted, "Fuck you."

"Oh. Don't worry yourself about that. The bill is coming your way at five-hundred an hour."

CHAPTER 13

Outside of the Round House's cell block, Dotty rushed towards the exit's swinging door and it slammed into her face by a cop entering the building. It was the cop who had spoken with Dotty two mornings ago while she sat in Lynch's hearse next to Sister Tudor.

"Are you OK, ma'am?" The officer asked and warmly placed a hand on Dotty's shoulder.

She covered the bottom of her face, blood leaked from her nose onto her fingers, which were badly in need of a manicure. In a high-pitched voice, she said, "Oh yes, Sir, I am being great, very very great, thank you."

"You don't look all that great."

"I'm great. I always look this way, Sir." Bowing with exaggeration she pulled open the door to flea the police HQ.

"Wait, ma'am. We've met, right?"

"Absolutely not. I would be very very sure had we met. I'm sure."

THE DRUNK DETECTIVE

Outside she leaned against a Channel Six Action News van and blew her nose into some tissue from a reporter. She was occupied cleaning up when a red Dodge Charger pulled into the space behind the van. It's driver put down the passenger window and leaned to look out of it. "Hey, Dotty, you OK?"

"Oh yes, I am just great, very very..." She noticed that it was Naim Butler and her tune changed. "Oh, it's you. I'm good."

"When your cell kept going to VM, I called Goldberg and he told me to call Rodriguez who told me you'd been arrested. Why?"

"Right now, I shouldn't discuss the case. You know, pending investigation red-tape. I'm out for now, can I get a ride?"

"That's why I showed up. Where you going?"

"Find a parking lot. In fact, go to the big one on Market Street between Eighth and Ninth across from the Gallery Mall."

"Do I look like an UBER driver?"

"For now, yes."

They rode for a few blocks in silence. The Charger's engine purred and the tires hissed on the dewy streets. Dotty went through her pockets until she found the pigskin-and-gold notebook she'd removed from the front of Our Lady of the Rosary Church's rectory. She had assumed that perhaps the bishop had dropped it on his way in, but now she guessed the killer dropped it on their way out.

The first five pages were filed with names and numbers recorded in the same print that had sent her an invite to the first meeting. Presumptuously, the bishop's neat script. Dotty recognized some of the local church celebrities, the ones that were questioned on TV about a sex scandal. There were some city officials, and local area celebs, but most were unknown to her. There was a lone number on a page with a 202-area code: Washington, DC.

Naim pulled into the parking lot as Dotty dialed the DC number. Oddly, she felt like some kind of capped-sleuth who had to get to the bottom of a bishop's murder and the almost-murder of a prostitute. This for one simple reason, the bishop was going to pay Dotty's bills for the next thirty years or longer.

"United States Justice Department."

It was a pleasant kind of voice. Dotty said, "Thee US Justice Department in Washington?"

"The one and only, ma'am. Can I help you?"

"Well are we talking the state or the place with the big white buildings?"

"The state of Washington, ma'am, doesn't have a just department. They have rain."

"OK, let me get the man at the top. The Big Cheese."

"You mean the woman, Attorney General, Loretta Scalia."

Dammit, man. "Well, if she's available, yes."

"Your name?"

"Just tell her the City of Brotherly Love is calling."

"Okey-dokey. One moment, City of Brotherly Love."

Dotty was placed on hold. After some elevator music bored her, a raspy, university-loaded voice she knew vaguely from television broadcasts came on the line.

"Lynch, I told you to never call me here." She hung up.

Dotty tossed her phone on the dashboard, and said, "Wow."

THE DRUNK DETECTIVE

"What happened? Who was that?"

"The Justice Department. Seems they're in on this Church killing spree. I'm wondering the connection to Frankie Robinson now."

"Where to next?"

"You can't hang wit me, kid. I'm dangerous right now."

"You were yesterday, too. And the days and months before that." He started the car, and then turned to Dotty. "Let me thank you for the advice. Scott Dempsey was in a hotel room with a dirty blonde. He came clean about the thefts. Mr. Goldberg gave me a bonus."

"I bet he loved that."

"He acted like I was problematic. But he made up the bonus rule, so he had to pay up. He had the audacity to put a reprimand in my file for violating his other company rule."

"Screw his rules. If his reprimands were bullets, I'd be Swiss cheese."

"That wasn't a compliment. I invested the money with a Wall Street broker already. I've got big ambitions, Dotty."

Dotty's spider-senses perked up. "I see you know how to prioritize. Glad I could be of service to your goals." Naim began to back out of the space. Dotty cracked a window. "What are you going to do now?"

"I am still wondering."

"Do not do that. It's dangerous and hurts the brain."

"Let me tag along with you on this case. You can teach me some pointers. You know about being a great investigator."

"There's no case. I don't even have a job."

"You can work for yourself. You don't need an agency."

"I just got out of jail."

"Many great woman went to jail. Men sleuths, too. Sherlock Holmes..."

"A wuss. He didn't do anything and they'd have his ass at the Round House, too. Anyway, he's fictional."

"No shit, Sherlock. I was just hoping."

"I don't know, kid." Dotty said and popped in a toothpick. "Maybe there is something you can help me with. I've read something in your personnel file."

"Perfect. What's that?"

"Hold up, don't get your panties pooped in. No pay, just experience."

"What you need me to do?"

Dotty smiled. "You know why you were arrested in Chicago. I need that expertise."

CHAPTER 14

"Get away from me, Dotty," Swayze said, sitting in a semi-circular booth in the Circ Restaurant inside of the downtown Marriott Hotel. He wore a white bib with a Maine lobster on it, and the remains of the same life form lay on his plate, classical music played very low in the background.

"Your secretary told me that I could find you here. I need your help."

"Tell my secretary she's fired. Who's this with you?"

"Naim Butler. He's an intern with the agency from U of Penn Law School."

"Hello, sir," Naim said. "I've heard so much about you."

"You bitch," Swayze said to Dotty. "It had better been all nice. I see no one has killed you, yet." Swayze picked out some of the lobster's brain with a miniature fork.

"That's why we're here."

"Oh, I'll kill you after I'm done with the lobster."

"Such a comedian, Swayze." Dotty and Naim slid into the booth and a waiter handed them menus. "Isn't you got any cheap burgers?"

"The ground sirloin here is good," Naim said. "And it's *don't*, ma'am."

"You can afford it. A firm sent you here from New York and pay for your Ivy League schooling. I'm sure they're paying for you to have fine dining. I don't have that luxury." She returned her menu to the waiter, and said, "I'll have what he just praised. Well done with a slice of Velveeta. None of that provolone crap."

"And to drink?"

"What's on tap?"

"There's a full assortment of imported beers."

"Nothing from Mexico. It makes me piss all damn day, and mine is just starting this late. Bring me a Corona in a can. I found a nose hair in a bottle once," she confided to Swayze and Naim. "What do you think, he does it to the busboy, or the busboy does it to him?"

"Jesus Christ, Dotty." That was Naim. "You can't be homophobic."

"You see the way those hips sway when they carry trays. Waiting tables was made for a woman." She took a gulp of Swayze's water. "So here's what I need from you two."

"Oh boy," Swayze said.

"Look, you're still a whiz with computers?"

"Never was."

"That's why Naim is here. He was in jail for hacking credit card numbers from Chance Bank. Did hard fed time, now he's on track."

"There is a God," Swayze said.

Dotty said, "We need to use a computer at your job."

"Why the hell is that?"

"Simply put. To bust into the files at the Justice Department. The Chinese do it, so can Mr. Butler, here."

"You're talking about the Justice Department in Washington, D.C.?"

"They don't have one in Washington state. I asked. They have rain."

"You idiot."

"Oh well, I've been called worse. I need to know why the AG would want to kill a male prostitute and a bishop, and what it all has to do with a dead nun."

"Loretta Scalia, as in the first African-American female AG with an Italian last name?"

"That's funny, right?"

"Their files. I can break into them," Naim said.

Dotty's ground sirloin came, on a big plate with a kid's portion of broccoli and wild rice?" Dotty asked. "People pay twenty-eight-dollars for this. Am I supposed to eat it or take a picture of it and post it on Instagram?"

"You have an Instagram?" Naim asked in spite of himself.

"You can shove it up your rude ass for all I care." The waiter left.

"He gets no tip," Dotty told Swayze. "He forgot my beverage."

"You said that like you ordered a Sprite."

THE DRUNK DETECTIVE

"Why do you like the attorney general for murder?" Swayze asked.

"When I called there, because I found the number in a notebook that I stole from Bishop Sinclair..."

"You're going straight to hell."

"...I said it was the City of Brotherly Love calling, Scalia came on the line and called me Lynch." Dotty spoke whole chewing ground sirloin. "Lynch is the one that booby-trapped the gigolo's apartment. That will be on tonight's news thanks to Naim who's banging a production assistant there."

"Dotty!"

Swayze said, "That was on the radio this morning. Cops claim to have a suspect awaiting arraignment."

"That was me, you dope. I was sprung not to long ago. So can we use the computer?"

"The AG has all kinds of server security codes, I doubt lover boy here can get in as easily as he gets into pants."

"See that, Dotty. You're giving people the wrong impression of me."

"He can. Did you know last month a teenager obviously bored in Lincoln, Nebraska tapped into the Pentagon and sent a thousand cases of Magnum condoms and KY-Jelly to Syria."

"Quite the international care giving effort it it cuts down on the number of little Islamic State babies being born," Swayze said.

"This is about money, Swayze," Naim said.

"Yup," said Dotty. "If the bishop was willing to pay on his low wages, what do you think a member of the president's cabinet would pay up. All them assholes down there want to be president."

"Have you asked yourself why Scalia would care how a Philly priest kicked the bucket?"

"That's why I need to help Dotty hack into the AG's E-mails. It's hard to blackmail someone without the goods," Naim said.

"This could be a million pay out," Dotty said.

"Dollars," Naim added. "Hell, BMWs."

"From this moment on it's all fifty-fifty," Dotty said.

Swayze raised his eyebrows. "You cross me, Dotty-O-Pal, and I'll have your ass for breakfast."

"I would never stiff a friend. I resent the accusation." Dotty finished her meal and stood. Naim followed suit. "Don't forget what I said about the tip."

* * *

Naim dropped Dotty off at her apartment. She planned to have him pick her up later near closing time for Swayze's bank, so that they could slip into the back door and do what they had to do. Sitting on the front steps of her apartment building was Hank Robinson in a puffy Eagles NFL jacket, complimentary fitted ball cap pulled down to his eyebrows, and gaudy sunglasses.

Dotty said, "I didn't recognize you. Thought you were a thug rapper."

He laughed. "I didn't know that you lived next door to a sleazy massage parlor."

"Now you do. What are you doing here?"

"Waiting on you. I really need to talk to you," he said, and looked deeply into her eyes.

THE DRUNK DETECTIVE

"Well, I am all ears. Let me go straighten up my apartment. It's a mess. I'll all you in a sec to come on up."

Racing to her apartment, Dotty got right to straightening up her apartment. She put chairs and tables upright, flipped over damaged cushions to disguise the holes. She even mopped with some disinfectant, something that she never did. Finally, she emptied the dregs of four different kinds of liquor from nine bottles into a tall glass and gulped that down her throat. The empties went into a garbage bag with the rest of the trash, and then out of a window aimed at a dumpster in the alley. It landed with a thud, sending a cat scurrying and just missing a bum. She then went downstairs, to collect her guest. The dregs had provoked her appetite; the steak did nothing.

* * *

Upstairs, Hank gasped at the door to Dotty's lair.

"Bad termite problem," she said, unlocking it.

He went in first and walked through a path that Dotty had cleared to her bedroom. He reached for the light switch, Dotty screamed, "No!" and grabbed his bicep. She sniffed for gas before flipping the switch. "Can't be to careful," she said.

"My place never looked this bag on campus as a freshman. You need a man.

"What're you, broccoli?" she asked at the bedroom door.

"I mean to clean for you. This place looks like it's been ransacked."

"It could use a light dusting." She picked up a destroyed pillow, releasing a cloud of feathers into the air. "You thirsty/"

"A little. What you have?"

She lifted a bed sheet and a bottle with liquid in it popped into the air. She caught it, opened it, and smelled. "Looks like vodka."

"I'll take it. What I want to do, I shouldn't be sober for." His tone slipped to seductive and she turned to face him. "Let's drink this." He took the bottle from her.

* * *

It was light outside when Dotty rolled out of the bed onto her hands and knees, grabbed the dresser to stand, and stumbled naked to the bathroom. She flicked on the light and looked absurdly at herself in the mirror above the sink. Her breasts hung down near her stomach and were depressingly flat. Her skin tone was pale and pink-colored. She threw water on her face, before a quick wash over her pertinent parts, and then crept back into the bedroom.

She kicked the door and stubbed a toe and bit down on her lip to avoid screaming. She was deathly afraid of waking Hank, who was breathing heavily on his back with his eyes shut and the sheet pulled down exposing a chiseled chest and stomach. He looked serene and ready for another round. *This must run in the Robinson family*, she thought. Immediately after Dotty gathered herself, she put his fitted cap on her head. She smiled looking in the mirror at herself.

When she was done parading around in the mirror on her dresser, he said, "Having fun?"

"I night buy one of these. We'll be twinning. Or to wear to the Eagles games, of course."

He chuckled.

"What's funny?" she asked, sitting the hat down on the dresser.

"You are. When you're naked."

She sat on the side of the bed, and smiled at him. "Well, I don't hit the Zumba classes or run. I own a car."

"I meant the hat."

She grinned. "Oh, good thing I took it off."

He sat up and pulled on his boxers. He checked his watch, and then shot off the bed. "Shit."

"What's wrong?"

"I had a class this afternoon. I have to go."

"It's not polite to eat and run," she said. "Come back to bed."

"I really can't. I have to get to a class late."

"I understand," she said, and then slipped in her clothing, too. "I guess I better let you go."

"We'll meet up again. Call me."

"You never got around to telling me why you came here in the first place."

"Well, you've taken my mind off my problems, and I don't even know why I came. Glad that I did stop by, though." He winked at her. "Bye, Ms. Dotty."

Hank left and she decided to straighten up her apartment. *He may come back. I did put it on him.* After minimal work, she became hungry, and said, "Fuck this shit. He can do this. That is what he said. I gotta eat to pack back on those calories that I lost."

She dressed—ugly X-mas sweater and pajama bottoms, loafers without socks—and walked out of the door.

"Good afternoon, Mrs. Lombardo," she said as she spun around the second floor landing.

The blind bat was perched at the bottom of the stairs looked up, fixed her glasses on her nose, and pointed a pale finger. "That's her!"

Then Dotty saw the officer who had seen her in the car with Sister Tudor and the same one that busted her nose. In front of them the door of Chen's apartment where Dotty had stashed his body was ajar. The officer un-holstered his revolver.

"Freeze!"

He had sounded like a TV cop, and Dotty guessed that's where he's gotten the line. No criminal had ever froze on that command. Obviously, innocent people didn't freeze either, Dotty turned around and was running up the stairs she'd just came down. The police officer gave chase.

On her floor, Dotty didn't bother to try to locate her keys, she said eff this and went through what was left of the door. The window used for a trash shoot by her a moment ago was still open.

Without second guessing, she climbed over the sill, was perched there for a second, then as soon as she heard the footsteps enter her place she pushed off. She was a woman without wings, but flew for two seconds. Then she slammed into the ground with her knees in her chest, on top of a dead rat, the cat she scared away earlier may have caught and all but one of the bottles she had thrown out moments before.

When she was able to refocus, she saw a homeless woman right outside the dumpster. The woman had the other bottle tipped upside down and was rubbing at the insides of the neck with a crusty tongue. Dotty recognized her as a panhandler outside of the McDonald's on Market Street.

THE DRUNK DETECTIVE

The woman popped her lips and balled up her face. "You actually drank this piss?" she asked.

CHAPTER 15

The only jarring difference between the woman and Dotty worth noting was the woman's jacket was a green and yellow Green Bay Packers number covered in a patina of filth. Dotty's blazer was a more conservative black polyester.

"You got a hover board or something 'cause you get around the Center City area, I see," Dotty said. "I thought bums stayed closer to where they ate and panhandled."

"Who the hell you calling a bum? Do I look like a bum? I am not any body's bum."

"What are you, Ms. Universe?"

"When the Christmas lights get put away, I am homeless."

"OK, Homeless, can you drive a car?"

"Is Putin a communist?"

"I take that as a yes."

"I wasn't always like this."

THE DRUNK DETECTIVE

"Homeless, I have twenty easy bucks for you. Wanna make a quick buck?"

"Did Martin Luther King win a Nobel Peace Prize?"

"You must get rest in the main library on Vine."

"Yup, you can find me between African-American studies and Russian History on Monday's," she said, smiling with five teeth that had never been close to each other.

Dotty held up a twenty-dollar-bill. "Let's exchange jackets."

Homeless looked skeptically, put down the empty bottle and felt one of Dotty's lapels between thumb and forefinger. "I'm used to foreign wool and Asian denim," she said. "But OK."

They switched outerwear and Dotty handed her the bill and the car keys. "There's a fancy Mercedes parked in front of this apartment building. Get to it and burn rubber. Someone will chase you."

"Cops or robbers?"

"Cops."

"OK, I don't mess with the South Philly Italian mob. Where should I leave it?"

"How 'bout Canada? I don't care, it ain't mine and the owner has much bigger problems." Dotty heard keys and the squawk of a walkie-talkie entering the alley. "Get out of here."

Homeless shrugged, flicked a banana peel off the sleeve of Dotty's blazer, and jumped over the dumpster. Dotty heard the officer shout, "Freeze!" again and then there were galloping footsteps. A shot rang out and made the dumpster ring as loud as the Liberty Bell. She then heard more police footsteps.

She backed against a wall and then jumped inside the dumpster as the cops ran by. She heard the Mercedes revved up and burned rubber.

Ten minutes passed before, she grabbed the top of the dumpster and peeked over the side. The cat that she had scared off earlier hissed at her between licking the interior of a discarded tuna can. Otherwise she was alone. She climbed out. The loud jacket had began to make her itch. At the length of the alley she came out on Spring Garden Street, where a few cabs passed her up until a Saudi with an expired VISA driving a newer Yellow Cab stopped for her.

"I gotta get twenty up front, ma'am, to take you any where."

Dotty dug into her pocket and showed him some cash. She handed the driver a ten.

"Where to, ma'am? 'Cause this won't get you far."

Dotty hesitated. She had time to kill before she was supposed to meet Swayze in a city with cops that were tracking her for murder. "U of Penn," she said. "I'll tell you where to drop me exactly when we get over there."

"That's normally how it works."

For Dotty the ride across downtown was magical. She was whisked by corporate buildings that ran along JFK Boulevard until they reached 30th Street Station, all the while the cab driver (a devout Muslim) avoided blasphemies while cursing every driver that cross lanes or turned without using a signal. As she text Naim Butler, they shot over to Market Street and passed Drexel University before they reached the University of Penn Law Library with a cop car just a car behind them. She had him pull over with the meter reading: $9.75.

THE DRUNK DETECTIVE

"Keep the change," she said leaving the driver a quarter tip for his harboring a fugitive.

She walked a block up Walnut Street to Naim's dorm and he was waiting in the lobby for her. When he noticed the Green Bay Packers jacket he cringed.

"Where to, ma'am? 'Cause this won't get you far."

Should've gotten an Uber. Dotty hesitated. She had time to kill before she was supposed to meet Swayze in a city with cops that were tracking her for murder. "U of Penn," she said. "I'll tell you where to drop me exactly when we get over there." *Just in case you're an operative.*

"That's normally how it works."

"Just drive, asshole."

For Dotty the ride across downtown was magical. She was whisked by corporate buildings that ran along JFK Boulevard until they reached 30th Street Station, all the while the cab driver—a devout Muslim—avoid blasphemies while cursing every driver that crossed lanes or turned without using a signal. As she text Naim Butler, they shot over to Market Street and passed Drexel University, before they reached the University of Penn Law Library. With Dotty's luck, a cop car pulled behind them. She had him pull over with the meter reading $9.75.

"Keep the change," she said, leaving the driver a quarter tip for his harboring an innocent fugitive.

She walked a block up Walnut Street to Naim's dorm and he was and he was waiting in the lobby for her. When he noticed the Green Bay Packers jacket, he cringed. "You need to get rid of the jacket. In Eagles Nation you stick out a lot and with the whole PPD gunning for you, I doubt you want that kind of attention."

"Keep it down. Jesus," she said, tossing the jacket on a seat in the lobby as they walked to a corner with a bank of pay phones. "Do these work?"

"Yes." He was laughing.

"Anything to drink?"

"Vending machines. All Pepsi products."

"Pepsi? I was thinking more like bourbon or vodka."

"I'm not a drinker. I could go get you hard liquor, though."

"Hard liquor. You're such a nerd. Don't bother," she said, eyeing every student suspiciously as they ebbed through the lobby to their dorm rooms.

"OK, so what's the plan? My head is full of Child Psychology after class."

"Mine, too. What time is it? My watch was ruined breaking my fall from grace."

"Nearly five."

They turned to the thirty-six inch screen TV on the wall. The news fanned a BREAKING NEWS banner across the screen, interrupting Barb "Hurricane" Smith's weather predictions. "This just in…" said the anchor.

"Dotty?"

"Quiet."

"The owner of an adult massage parlor…"

"Is there any other kind?"

"…was discovered dead in his apartment an hour ago, the victim of what appears to be strangulation. Lee Chen, age seventy-four…"

"What now, Dotty?"

THE DRUNK DETECTIVE

"Hush, Naim."

"...a tenant, who called police. Police sought a suspect from the apartment building, who fled and escaped in a new model blue Mercedes..."

"Dotty! I thought you were in a taxi?"

"...suspect's name hasn't been released. We will have more, but now for our update with the sex party at the home of the Temple U lacrosse team." The anchor's face dissolved to a close-up of a beat reporter outside of the team's home holding a box of Lifestyle condoms.

'You didn't do him, did you?" Naim asked.

"No, I ain't been to Temple U in years."

"You know I am talking about Chen. You need to grow up."

"Some murdered named, Lynch, I been telling you about did the old man. The old bag from my building saw me moving the body."

"Oh, wow. Today?"

"A day ago, My bad, this just never came up in conversation."

"You're funny. What about the gigolo? He talking?"

Dotty scratched her left elbow. "You got Lysol around here. I need to get rid of these germs."

"No. Answer my question, Dotty."

She shrugged. "I'm not sure."

"This is crazy. How'd the hell you go from being a drunk detective—well, PI—to being involved in all of this?"

"I detect some shade in that comment, hun bun. Simple. A damn nun sewed her royal oats in a Mandingo warriors bed

in my building. I got rid of her. Quietly, by the way. Now this Lynch clown wants to get rid of me, but Chen got in the damn way."

"Why not just tell the police all of this?"

"Too problematic. Chen was strangled in my apartment. I found him, and kindly took him to his place."

"Doesn't look good. But, hey, I'm just in law school."

"Who you telling?"

"You moved two dead bodies and told the police about neither. I mean, I am no lawyer, but my TV lawyer instincts are telling me you're in deep shit."

"Would you have told on yourself?"

"I'm a black ex-con with a rap sheet worthy of praise. Imagine it."

"Look, Butler, the bishop is dead, too. I'm pretty sure, Loretta Scalia sicced Lynch on Chen, Frankie and the bishop, but I don't know why. We will find out when you get into Scalia's computer."

"Let's do this," he said, looking at his watch. "It's that time. Wait here while I grab my car from the garage. Don't need anyone seeing you roaming the campus. They have that facial recognition crap included with the surveillance.

Just as Naim walked away, Dotty was approached by Hank Robinson.

"What are you doing here, Hankie Pankie?" she asked, fixing her hair.

"I should ask you that. I go to school here, remember?"

"Right. I found out some things about who may be responsible for hurting your brother. Turns out," she said, covering

her mouth, "well, I can't tell you right now, but I will say that there's a chance that DC is involved."

"Who's he?"

"The Government."

"Oh, Big Brother. That's fair, my brother hasn't filled out a W-2 in ages."

She giggled. "Ok, but this isn't about him not paying taxes in years. It could be apart of the problem, though." She heard a car horn and looked out and saw Naim waving at her. "I have to go."

"OK, but please find out who hurt my brother."

"I'll keep you posted."

"You have the Post-It already?" He smiled.

She blushed. "As a matter of fact, I do," she said, winked and then backed up. "I gotta run." She turned around and ran out of the building. Out of the corner of her eye she saw the Green Bay Packers jacket walking up the street. Someone pushing a shopping cart was wearing it.

CHAPTER 16

Refer to her as Dotty.

Better yet, don't refer to her for any reason, and definitely if it's not about money. Calling her before noon, despite her profession, was also out of the question. If you do she's undoubtedly going to answer on the fourth ring and say something like: "I don't know you and your call may be important, but at this time it's not. Please, do the police a favor, hang up right now, or I will hunt you down and drain your car's brake fluid."

The caller sighed. "Too bad I don't own a car."

"Then I'll do something of remarkable relevance to you in the eyes of a coroner."

"Look, is this, Dotty?"

The voice was a low seductive one made for late night radio. Quite smooth. The last thing she wanted to hear was some catty woman at this hour. "Who the hell's calling?"

THE DRUNK DETECTIVE

"Frankie, ma'am."

"Doesn't ring a bell."

"Frankie Robinson. I live in the apartment right below you, for crying out loud. We speak every day."

"The male stripper? Sometimes gigolo?"

"Um, Dotty, you live over a Chinese owned massage parlor known to give happy endings. What do you expect for a neighbor, a damn neurosurgeon?"

Dotty sat up in her twin-sized bed and ran a hand through her elephant-colored hair. Her hair was course and dry. She fished around her nightstand and found a Mickey Mouse watch. She angled it to see its face using the light making its way into her bedroom from the massage parlor's outside signage. She sat the watch down and whined into the receiver, "It's three-thirty a-damn-m."

"Gee, all of my clocks stopped, so I called you for the time. Thanks. Look, you're some kind of detective lady, correct?"

"Not at this time of the morning."

"I'll give you five-hundred bucks to come down to my apartment right now."

She drew a deep breath. "Shouldn't I be offering you money?"

"What the fuck, Dotty. Can you come down or not? You ain't the only detective with breasts in town. I only called you because you could get here the quickest."

"What's your problem? You have to have one."

"As a matter of fact, I do have a dead nun in my bed. And Dotty that is a huge fuckin' problem."

* * *

When the he-bitch repeated himself, she said that she was heading right down and hung up. She sat there and ran her tongue across her front teeth. They felt like they were covered in dust. When she threw back her blanket, a round brandy bottle popped into the air. She tried catching it, but realized it was empty, and let it drop to the floor. She slipped on tattered slippers and ambled to a cluttered bathroom, which wasn't going to change. She plopped on the toilet to empty her bladder, while engaged in her morning routine, asking herself:

"What's your name? Dorothy Davis."

"And where do you live? I don't freakin' know."

"Where did you drink last night? Oh, come on."

One out of three wasn't bad. Hell, that was better than usual.

Back in the bedroom she fell onto the bed and pulled her hair into a sloppy ponytail and after scanning the floor she found a pair of jeans. These she slipped over pink cotton pajamas, which peeked out at the bottom of her pant legs. She slid on Christmas themed argyle socks and pushed them into penny loafers with dimes in them. It was February so she tugged on a puffy jacket, grunting with the effort. She was fifty-six, overweight, strong as a bull. She looked for her semi-automatic simply because it was 3:30 a.m. in downtown Philadelphia, but she was wasting her time; she hadn't seen it in weeks. She forgot about it and headed out. The hallway smelled of incense, condoms, and collard greens.

Frankie Robinson's buzzer actually worked. None of the other tenants did, and the landlord didn't care one iota. The door creaked open. Frankie's head was just below the top of the door frame. He was shirtless in red boxer briefs and neat dreadlocks rested on his shoulders.

THE DRUNK DETECTIVE

"You look ridiculous," he said.

"I'm running on three hours sleep. I see why the ladies love you, though. Where's my five hundred?"

"Don't you want to see the body first?"

"Hell no. Do I look like a lesbian?"

"Don't make me answer that." They stepped away from the doorway and he removed a painting from the wall revealing a safe. He opened it, pulled out some cash and pushed five hundred into Dotty's palm. He put the rest back, locked the safe and replaced the painting.

"I thought you kept your money in the nightstand where the broads leave it for you after sordid sex." She scanned the bills and then pocketed them.

"Funny. Mine is hidden for creeps like you that think they know everything."

He locked the front door and led her through a cramped living room styled by an IKEA rep into a tiny bedroom containing a queen-sized water bed that took up ninety-percent of the room. The other ten was occupied by Sister Anne Tudor, principal of Our Lady of Rosary, the Catholic school that prepared her daughter for college.

For the first time she saw the sister's curves sans her religious habits. Mother Superior's face was rosy and her mouth was curved into a smile. She died happy.

Dotty fished into her jacket pocket for a toothpick and stuck it into her mouth. She twirled it around and was beginning to feel better already. "She a constant client?"

"Loose lips, sinks my future. I don't kiss and report it. I thought that she was breathing heavy. Then she wasn't at all."

"Welp, she's deader'n Mother Theresa."

"Once again, thank you. I thought she was mimicking a fucking BMW."

"At least she's no lesbo." She tossed a hand on her lips. "Let me guess, you have no idea where I was at last night do you?"

He furrowed his brow and slapped a hand on her shoulder. "You wouldn't be up if you had been here, Dotty. I assure you."

"I'll recall soon enough. What do you actually want me to do?"

"Get her the hell out of here, what else? Cops find a nun's body here, I'll lose my nicely set up tax-free enterprise."

"Five more hundred."

"Get the fuck outta here. I just gave you five bills."

"So. That was to show my pretty face. You're lucky I don't charge by the pound. Look at those hips and that gut. Geesh."

"{You} look the hell at it. She's on her back because she liked it missionary. I had to climb on that."

"And you call this a nice enterprise. You're shitten me. What's five more hundred? You don't even flash your beef for that."

"You're a real comedian."

"So I've been told."

He walked out of the room and came back with five more hundred. She didn't count the money this time. "You need to leave for a while," she said. "Come back when the sun breaks with breakfast for two."

"Where the hell am I going this late?"

THE DRUNK DETECTIVE

"Pick a bed. Any bed. Give yours a break for a change. Go to a cocaine club. What? Am I a vacation planner? Use your brain for something besides giving brain."

"Son of a bitch." He ran his thumbs in the waist of his boxer briefs about to remove them, stopped. "You just going to stare at me? I only wore these for the sister."

"Is there a problem? Oh, payment. I'm broke."

"Get the hell out, lady."

"You should have told the nun that, before she died under you."

She got the hell out, slamming the bedroom door shut. In the living room, still working the toothpick, she drifted to the painting and removed it from the wall. The safe was locked. Frankie, in white boxers and a tank top, came out of the bedroom carrying a gun, put the painting back on the wall, and said, "I will kill you 'bout my money, Dotty." She admired his backside as he walked back into the bedroom.

Ten minutes later he emerged wearing jeans and a sweater that clung to his muscles. He was a dark skinned man, under thirty with boyish looks that authorized him to tell clients that he was nineteen. Cougars liked him young. He had a special trick that he did with his goatee that they liked also. Something about the way he handled himself made her wish she was a MILF.

"So where to?"

"A client's house. Gotta make my thousand bucks back by sunrise to be able to afford to bring you breakfast." He stopped at the front door. "What are you going to do with her?"

"Don't ask. You didn't want to tell me your dealings with her."

"Fuck you."

"Go fuck yourself."

When he had gone, she helped herself to a bottled Corona beer from the 'fridge in the kitchen. She drank another while looking up a number in her cell phone, as she headed back to the bedroom. She sat on the edge of the bed while waiting for someone to answer her call. She tapped the bed. "So, Sister. He worth the money?"

"You better believe it, honey."

Dotty spit out the toothpick, as the phone continued to ring. She cleared her throat. "Is this Our Lady of the Rosary parish?"

"Yes, this is Bishop Sinclair. It's four, you know?"

"Thank you. The name's Dorothy Davis. I'm a private dick, I mean, detective. I'm sorry."

"You should be."

"I'm also sorry to inform you that Sister Tudor is dead."

"Jesus Christ." The irritation left his voice. "How? What happened?"

"I'm not a doctor. But I think it's heart related."

"Virgin Mary Mother of God. In bed?"

"How'd you guess?" She held back inappropriate laughter.

"Was she...Could she have been in a state of grace?"

Dotty pulled out another toothpick. "Now you see why I'm calling at four a.m., Bishop Sinclair," she said and added, "we really need to talk."

THE DRUNK DETECTIVE

CHAPTER 17

What a place to die. "It had better been worth it." When she was through chastising the nun, she phoned the massage parlor downstairs. It rang and rang until a voice like gravel being ground picked up.

"What the hell. Hello."

"Chen, this is Dotty."

"So. It's four thirty a.m."

"Appreciate it. I'm up at Frankie's sex room."

"Must be nice?" There was a chuckle in his voice.

"I need to borrow your camera. It records, too, right?"

Pause. "Who you going to get to take the shots of you two? I sure as hell ain't."

"Cut it out. Bring it up to me."

"Um. What about the back rent?"

"I have two hundred for you right now. I just need to borrow the camera."

"You should also give me whatever you planned on paying the play boy horse. Besides, the last time you borrowed something I saw it at a pawn shop."

"It was swiped from my car. How many times we have to go over this?"

"You pawning something of mine, missing or being late with my rent due dates the last twelve years or more?"

"Look its to early. I need the camera."

"Use your cell phone."

"Can't. It's a dated flip phone. You going to give it to me or not?"

"Frankie's giving it to you."

"Sad."

"You got five hundred bucks?"

"Hell no. The camera isn't even worth that much."

"Already thinking of how much you can sell it for, eh?"

"No, man."

"OK, you have two hundred cash?"

"Yes, what you think I was going to use my Amex Black Card?"

"Just checking. Last time you wrote me a check, it bounced from here to Shangai. My father caught it there."

"Chen."

"I'll be up. Have the cash in your greasy palms."

THE DRUNK DETECTIVE

Dotty hung up. Conversations with her landlord was like playing tennis in a fish bowl. Without thought she pocketed an expensive watch she found on the night stand.

Chen sounded like a NFL commentator and looked like a house in a town called Pleasantville with his neatness. He was anything but. He had an emaciated square frame, perfectly bald head, bold eyes, a square nose, and when he walked his feet pointed outward like a penguin's. Old age had claimed his hair; Dotty had a bet with a bookie that Chen had a bald crotch, but neither had had any real motivation to find out to win the bet. He stood in the hallway wearing a lint covered pajama set and dangling the camera, a new Polaroid, from its strap at his side. "My money?"

Dotty had the two hundred separated from her eight and laid two in the landlord's skinny palm.

"I don't know where you got the loot. But before you spend it all tricking, remember you owe me six more hundred."

"Give me this."

He gave it to her. "Where's the horse?"

"Out. Working."

"I thought this was a home based business? No?"

"Not right now." Dotty turned on the camera. "You didn't see me head out last night, did you?"

"Watched you go and return. It was after midnight. You look ridiculous, by the way."

"Did I return with anyone?"

"Yes, as a matter of fact you did. Kat William and Kevin Hart. How could you forget their company? The lucky charm pimp and chocolate drop the rapper."

She hung her head low. "Good night, Chen. I'll return this later."

"You do that. I think I should come in and look around. It ain't like Frankie to be out this time of the morning. He could get raped by some crazy broad."

Dotty stepped in front of the door. "That would be theft of services. Get lost Chen. And don't forget to credit me the deuce."

Chen left and Dotty closed the door and locked it. She went through the photos on the camera and found salacious photos of the mayor and his mistress on several dates entering and exiting several suburban hotels. She had planned on making a buck off the sale of the photos to the mayor's wife, but she died of cancer rendering the photos worthless. She hated the city's corrupt politicians and sought to bring them all down on her spare time.

In the bedroom, she turned on the bedroom's overhead light and a bedside lamp illuminating Sister Tudor's bloated countenance. Her plumpness looked as if she was crying out loud in the confessional. Opening the closet, Dotty flipped through the clothing hanging there. Nothing suited what she looked for. She opened a drawer of the dresser and found several underwear types. She pulled out leopard print boxer briefs with Monday embroidered on the ass. She stepped back to survey the bed and then surmised the scene was too stuffy. She tossed the briefs on the bedpost with the day prominently displayed.

"There you go."

She took a series of pictures from many angles, finishing the photo shoot from the top of the bed that made the Sister look like an oversized Mona Lisa, then put the camera in her

THE DRUNK DETECTIVE

back pocket and went back to her apartment to stash it. Chen could take her to Judge Judy for it.

Back at Frankie's she put away her underwear prop, just then the door buzzer sounded.

"Dorothy Davis?"

The man ducked his head as he entered the apartment, with a complexion like damp clay and hair as white as snow, cropped close to his scalp. His feet were as huge as his hands with chewed-off fingernails. His black trench coat was dull.

"Yeah. You've been sent by the Bishop?"

"I'm Lynch."

The bishop had given him that name, and it may not have been real. She stepped aside and the tall man went straight to the bedroom without looking at anything else. Once there he looked at every aspect of the room.

"Awfully bright."

"I'm not used to being in the dark with a corpse," Dotty said.

"I have a time or two. Is there a fire escape?"

"Yup, but I doubt its been used since the Regan era. That's how long I've been living here. I wouldn't try to access it carrying a dead nun."

Lynch continued to admire the body. "She's bigger than I thought."

"You bring a dolly?"

"No." He lifted the nun's naked leg from the bed and let it drop. "Let's get her clothed while she's still flexible."

"You sound like a professional dead body remover. Why should we waste time dressing her?"

"It makes perfect sense to carry a naked body down two flights of stairs."

"Yeah, you must be a pro. What is it that you do for the bishop again?"

"I never said. The fee was three hundred." Dotty coughed up the money from her bra. A frosty hand touched Dotty's as the bills changed hands.

"Well let's do this."

The canoness' clothes consisted of black lace panties with a matching bra worn under her black tunic. She wore rosary beads around her neck. Lynch got the deceased left arm into a bra strap and, mumbling, lifted the upper body by the shoulders for Dotty to manage the other side. The nun groaned.

Dotty jumped to the other side of the room, slamming into the dresser. "She's alive!"

"That's just some left over air trapped in her lungs. They often do that. Hold her torso up, so I can slip on her panties." Next he covered her head and hair in her veil and coif.

Dotty apprehensively helped.

A half hour later passed before the nun was dressed and Dotty exchanged her disgust for exhaustion. They got her dressed, and then both put on a shoe and tied the laces.

Dotty dropped onto the bed and wiped her brow with her shirt sleeve. "If only my mother could see me. She always encouraged me to be closer to the Church."

"Top or bottom?"

She looked at Lynch, who still had on his coat, buttoned all the way up. "Do you sweat?"

"I wasn't paid for that. It'll be daybreak soon."

THE DRUNK DETECTIVE

"Yes, and I have breakfast coming."

Dotty took the head. They smoothly got the dead body into the hallway, and dragged it's heels across the runner onto the staircase landing, where they stood it against the wall. An old woman appeared at the bottom of the stairs, and started up carrying a handbag the size of Canada.

Dotty, kept the nun stable with a hand under her arm, smiled. "Good morning, Mrs. Lombardo. How was the casino?"

"I won, Dotty," she said two steps from the landing. "Every now and then Sugar House lets someone win. Who's that with you?"

"Just my buddy and his savior."

"She looks to need saving. She can barely stand up. My lips are sealed, because I don't like when the media airs out the Church's dirty laundry. I can understand a girl needing a drink, though. Don't let her drive."

"We're not, Mrs. Lombardo."

"She looks tore up from the floor up. Dead, in fact. She should've ate before drinking."

Dotty offered a strained smile. "Well, good night, Mrs. Lombardo."

"Good night, boys. And remember she can't drive." She continued to her apartment and locked herself inside.

"Mrs. Lombardo," Dotty told Lynch. "She was wasted herself."

"Think she's on to us?"

"She won't even recall this encounter in an hour."

"OK, let's get the Sister to the car. Give me a hand."

"Can't we just drag her down?"

"No. She'll get postmortem marks."

"Smart. Once again I ask, what do you do for the bishop." She began to be worried about her own well being and wished she had her gun.

The nun was stiffening. Dotty put her in a full-Nelson wrestling move--saying, "Lord, forgive me"--and, bearing a lot of weight backed down the stairs while Lynch held the feet in the air from snagging the heels on the shabby staircase runner. They stopped three times to rest. Dotty's nose was in Sister Tudor's collar for the trip down the stairs, long enough for her to develop a disdain for Chanel No. 5.

Just off the second landing, her foot slipped. She began to fall over, tried using the wall for leverage, managed to smash herself between the wall and her problem, said, "Jesus!" and let the nun go.

"Catch her, idiot." Lynch barked. Dotty caught her.

Executing a perfect curtsy, the nun tipped forward down the stairwell with Dotty embracing her from the back. They fell down the steps and landed in the tiled foyer, coming to rest against the door that led to the vestibule and sidewalk.

Lynch leaped down the stairs. "Great catch."

Dotty, sprawled on top of the corpse, said, "Now I have a damn pre-mortem bruise."

THE DRUNK DETECTIVE

CHAPTER 18

The car parked in front of the massage parlor's front door was a charcoal gray Cadillac; a big one mirroring a hearse. She stood in the doorway holding up the body while Lynch checked the street. She sighed and wished this whole ordeal was over with.

"Let's do it." Lynch was gaunt and barely alive as the nun under the dim light in the foyer. "Put her on the front passenger side."

"Huh? Why not the back seat? Lay her right across it."

"Because then it'll actually look like a dead nun and not a sleeping one. You sure you're a detective?"

"Hell, let's put her behind the wheel. That'll be fun."

The passenger door was opened and they both tossed an arm on their shoulders and walked across the sidewalk--Dotty losing more breath with each step--sat her on the seat, got her feet inside, and positioning her upright before securing the seat belt, pulling it to its limits.

"Just marvelous." Dotty's voice was a high-pitched soprano.

"Make sure she doesn't go any where while I run upstairs to be sure everything is in order."

"Where the fucks she goin'? Opps. Sorry Sister."

"Just wait here. I can't believe this." Lynch went inside.

The night air was cold and whipping trash around the filthy downtown street. Dotty closed the nun's door and went around the back to sit in the driver's seat, closing the door. After a second or two, she let down the window. "You really splashed on the perfume tonight, honey." Just at that moment a police officer walked around the corner doing his rounds. The massage parlor was close to the Philadelphia Convention Center and its patrons were known to be robbed so police patrolled the area on foot for suspicious activity.

Dotty said O-fuck and looked for the car's keys, while sliding down in the seat. No such luck. The officer came over and shone a flashlight in her face.

"Does there seem to be a problem, ma'am?"

Dotty sat up. "No problem at all, sir. I'm just waiting on someone, he forgot his coat. Sir."

The officer shifted his flashlight past Dotty, who became moist under her armpits. "Ma'am is your other friend asleep or passed out?"

"Oh, this is my aunt June. I had to pick up my friend and was forced to bring her along so she wouldn't be left home alone. She's known to start fires."

The flashlight's angle shifted. Dotty leaned forward, then sat upright when the officer moved it out of her face. The

THE DRUNK DETECTIVE

beam shifted to the dead nun again, then darted back to Dotty, then back to the nun and rested there a long time.

"Does she need a doctor, ma'am? Is she a nun?"

"No and no sir, Officer, sir. She's schizophrenic and sometimes thinks she's a member of the Church. The meds had her knocked out cold. I told you she gets violent and starts fires if we don't dress her like this."

"Ma'am, are you being an ass by making fun of me by keep calling me, sir?"

"No, sir. I mean no. But you keep calling me ma'am. Just saying."

The officer shook his head. He was in his forties, with a square jaw and rough moustache and dull green eyes under the square visor of his cap.

"Wake her," he said.

"Please don't make me do that." She resisted another {sir.}

"No, I said wake her up. If you even can, 'cause she looks dead to my trained eye."

"Dead?" Dotty gave the officer a tortured grin. "Dead that's a good one. Ha-ha, dead."

"I wanna hear her laugh."

"Trust me, she lost her sense of humor when JFK was killed. That's what sent her over to the crazy side."

"Oh, really." The officer stepped back a few inches and groped his pistol. "Step out of the vehicle, ma'am."

Dotty had a terrible idea. Here goes nothing, she thought.

She slid her right arm behind the dead woman's back, saying, "Look alive, June. We're back home." She pushed the corpse's top half forward toward the dashboard. It moaned.

The officer chilled out, and took his hand off of his weapon.

"My apologies, ma'am. We have to be vigilant in the neighborhood. There are many weirdoes. No offense, ma'am."

"Yes, sir. I mean no sir. I mean no." Dotty had a firm grip on the nun's coat to keep her head from slamming into the dash. "I agree that you can't be to careful."

"It's just to protect us. You better get out of this area. She sounded awful."

"Yes sir."

"It's five-thirty a.m., you know?"

"Thanks, Officer."

The officer went on his merry way. Dotty let go of the nun and tossed a new toothpick in her mouth. Lynch appeared from the building with a sneer on his face.

"My God, what took you so long? A damn cop was here." Dotty got out of the car.

"I watched him. He smell a crime?"

"At first. I handled him, though. I gotta tell you, I haven't spent this much time with the clergy since I was baptized."

"You were raised a Christian?"

"My mother and father were devout Evangelicals. You know the ones all of the Republicans fight over for the presidential nomination. My husband tried converting me to the Catholic faith. It didn't take."

"Where is he now?"

"Alabama or Arkansas, or maybe it was Alaska. Definitely an {A} state."

"Divorced?"

"By now. I hope so. I'd hate to die and he get half of my apartment."

Lynch climbed into the driver's seat. "I guess this is where we say goodbye."

"What you plan to do with her?"

"You don't really even care."

"Lynch, I've known people fifteen years that I haven't been around this damn long."

"Well, it's over now." He slammed the door.

"Look, I'll keep it quiet."

Lynch started the engine. "What?"

"I said I'll keep quiet."

"Good for you." He rolled up the window and began to dial a number into his cell phone.

Dotty raced up to her apartment and took up position in her window to be sure that Lynch left with the nun. She watched him pull off and bend around the corner. She wondered if she should have waved goodbye; to Sister Tudor, not Lynch.

She had to be to work at nine a.m., but she wasn't tired any more. She played with the camera and looked at her handy work. She connected it to her computer and downloaded the pictures into a locked folder. The watch that she purloined from Frankie was a Rolex that she stuck in a desk drawer where she kept a bag of marijuana.

Yawning now, she curled up in bed at six a.m. and was feeling better. Her hangover had subdued--although she didn't recall where she had gotten wasted the night before-- she had five hundred dollars extra cash in her pocket, and pictures of a dead Catholic nun in a gigolo's bed. This was a great morning.

She woke up when a burly white fireman chopped through her apartment door with an axe.

"Where the hell is the fire?" asked the rookie fireman.

Dotty shot up and ran fingers through her hair. "That's my damn line."

"Wrong floor, Adam," someone yelled from the hallway. "Some prostitute's apartment below this one."

"My bad about the door ma'am." Adam ran out.

Dotty said, "Fuck" and looked for her jeans.

THE DRUNK DETECTIVE

CHAPTER 19

The arson investigator's name was Rodriguez.

His suit was blue and he had sweat running from his forehead that he kept wiping with a sooty handkerchief that left smudges. He was much smaller than the fireman that had chopped down Dotty's door and a couple of years younger than her. He wrapped a petite hand with blackened nails around Dotty's hand in greeting and ushered her out of the fried hallway into Frankie Robinson's apartment. To Dotty's dismay he lit a cigarette, dropped the match on the floor and the carpet smoldered.

What an idiot, she thought.

"Too much smoke in here."

"You don't say," she replied. "Smells like a bar-b-cue."

He blew smoke rings into the air.

"That would be the tenant. Know him at all?"

"We spoke on occasion. He OK?"

"At this point he should be getting worked on at the Burn Center of University of Penn Hospital in West Philly. They work miracles of Godly proportions there."

Perhaps, Sister Tudor was already an angel and looking over him, Dotty wished she could blurt.

"What's he do for a living?"

"Hook. What happened, I smell gas?"

"Could be that. He have any clients lately, well, last night?"

"That's how he gets the money to pay for the gas and other necessities, I presume."

"Can you describe any from last night?"

"I don't look at the broads. I hear them sometimes. The walls are thin. One of them could be the mayor's wife or something."

"What about any loud disturbances? You do live right above him."

"All arguments are loud, don't you think?" She fished in her pocket for a toothpick and found none. She pulled out her box of matchsticks to substitute, but thought better of it, given the company. "You think this was a purposeful act? Like someone tried to kill, Frankie?"

Rodriguez wiped his forehead. "Don't know the motive. You've been no help, Ms. Davis."

"You should be talking to Chen, the landlord. It's not my job to help you. You're the arson guru."

"I've talked to Chen. He was just as useless. By the way what is your job?"

"Private dick."

"Interesting. Than I'm sure you've paid far more attention to what's going on around here than you're letting on. You with an agency, or are you a loner like Dick Tracey?" He casually tapped live ashes onto the carpet. There was a little flame there, Dotty stamped out.

"Fuck Dick Tracey. He's fictional, sir. I work for Goldberg Discreet Inquirers on Broad and Arch Streets. I got to be there in a half hour." She had spent an hour in the hallway with other residents, watching firemen put out the fire and paramedics carry Frankie Robinson out covered in a white sheet. Chen found him balled into the fetal position on the wall opposite his apartment door, where the blast had shot him when he'd come home. Two platters of food lay beside him. Dotty was touched and had slept right through the explosion and the ensuing sirens. "And to be clear, if some nut job is blowing up my neighbors, I am privileged to the information."

"We've got no reason to believe that. I investigate arson leading to death. Does Frankie Robinson smoke?"

"He is now."

Rodriguez wiped his forehead, dropped the cigarette butt on the floor, and put away his tape recorder. "OK, that's all, I guess. Can I get a number to reach you?"

Dotty dug into her pocket and pulled out a few cards and gave him one engraved on red stock with a bouquet of white and yellow roses in the corner. The arson investigator furrowed his eyebrows. "A woman started the agency," Dotty said.

"Thanks for your time, Ms. Davis." Rodriguez opened the door for her.

Dotty left after stomping on the cigarette butt still smoking on the floor.

Dotty made her way back to the fourth floor and before she could get into her apartment Chen was on the fourth floor landing. With his hands in the pockets of his fuzzy pajamas and the dull hallway light shining on him.

"Not so fast, Dotty. What was you moving downstairs this morning after I gave you the camera, a load of bowling balls?" he asked.

Dotty expected the question to come from the arson investigator. "I had fell after slipping on that dated runner. You need to replace it."

"Where's your bruises? You had to have something break your fall."

"You sound like a cop. I have to get to work, Chen."

"Speaking of cops, I didn't tell the cops that you was the last person I saw in Frankie's place."

"Why not? The doll has not committed no crime."

"My camera?"

She covered her mouth and raised her eyebrows. "You know what. Funny story. It was in my car..."

"Look at this catastrophe." Chen was looking at the smoke covered walls. "I don't have money to redo these walls and my insurance won't cover arson unless someone is arrested and convicted for it. The cop's running around here are messing with the parlor's flow of traffic. People are discouraged from coming."

Dotty nodded. What could she say.

"Yup, that was a loud noise you made this morning with your skinny friend. I saw him," the landlord continued. He was now whispering. "I thought it was burglars, but I got a

THE DRUNK DETECTIVE

good view of you two through my peephole, Dotty. You were right on top of it. I hope I never get that huge."

"Look, get to the point, Chen."

"I'm old, not dumb. It was easy for me to put together an unknown man and a camera and a gigolo and a dead person dressed like a nun on the stairs. It'd be easy for the police, too. They tie those facts with the explosion and you have a problem bigger than any client you've ever had at Goldberg's."

"Arson crew called it a gas leak."

"And they may continue to believe that if you catch my drift."

"Chen, I don't get the drift at all."

"You got till tonight to get it. That's all the time I'll forget to give the cops these details. I want half your action, that's all I want. What's half? You decide and find me to discuss. You know I'm always here just like I was this morning. The peephole's a marvelous invention."

"I'm late for work, Chen."

Chen stepped out of her way. "Work won't matter if you're in jail, Dotty."

Dotty E-mailed the pictures to herself before heading out of her apartment and to work. She then changed her computer password and hid the camera. She didn't trust Chen and his key to her apartment.

* * *

The car she drove to work was a brand-new Mercedes S-series with cream guts. It belonged to a judge friend who had asked Dotty to sell it for her while she served a five-year sentence for taking bribes to alter criminal trial outcomes, only Dotty hadn't made time to sell it. The morning was the color of granite which matched the color of the over cast clouds, and the sun may not have been up. As she zipped around cars and pedestrians barely missing both, she thought about the explosion at Frankie's apartment. Although the building had had leaks in the past, she kept wondering what Lynch did for the bishop and what had he done during that lonely trip back up to the apartment without Dotty. {Coincidence, that's all a dick hopes for to close a file,} he mentor, old Donna Goldberg had said once. {When you record a man walking out of a house carrying a gasoline can and then the house goes up in flames, that check is as good as yours.} Except in that case the man with the can was a state representative and his wife was inside; which {had} been an accident. It had taken ten-thousand-dollars to stop the state rep from pressing charges for Dotty trespassing and leaking the footage to the local media. Regardless, it was sound advice.

Continuing her deep thoughts about the eruption, Dotty parked in a loading zone in front of the building on Broad Street and spent some time deciding which placard she wanted to prominently display in her window to avoid a ticket and tow. She selected VISITING CLERGY and said, "How appropriate," before she went into the building.

The gold letters on the wood doors to the floor where she worked read Goldberg Discreet Inquirers. The receptionist desk was shaped like a horseshoe and behind it was a male secretary who was really a guard in position to stop any crazies from coming in killing the investigator that exposed them. The glass coffee table was topped with spy and mystery magazines and paintings of fictional detectives covered the walls. It was an impressive sight which Dotty barely appreciated. She liked the old drab style before the makeover with PRESTIGE DETECTIVE AGENCY painted on the door.

THE DRUNK DETECTIVE

The receptionist was in a tight suit and his muscles were about to pop the threads.

"Morning, Jack," Dotty said. "You ought to lay off the steroids and performance enhancement drugs. I can imagine how small your phallus has gotten."

He didn't look up from the Philadelphia Daily News. "Mr. Goldberg wants you in his office."

"What he want this time around, my luscious body?"

"Just your heart. He asked me to send in the dickhead as soon as she shows up."

"You're kidding right? How'd you assume he meant me?"

"This agency is like a pair of trousers. Only one dickhead can fit in them at a time." He turned the page.

She smiled and leaned into him, whispering, "The Roosevelt Inn rents by the hour. How 'bout it?"

He finally looked up from the newspaper, frowned, and gave her a look to kill. "How 'bout a sexual harassment charge?"

"Gym rats. Never a direct answer." She shrugged and went through the door behind the desk.

She meandered down the short hallway fixing her clothes along the way. A cheap, barely pressed, business suit didn't do much for her personality but it was the attire for the office. She checked her hair in a wall mirror, which was out of the ponytail and a strategic mess before she knocked on the bosses door. She was wearing her lucky ascot, an expensive Versace number left in the glove box of her judge friend's car. She was serving time, so had no need for it.

"Come in, Dotty."

The office was huge and decorated with a masculine tone, black carpet, white walls, and a glass desk. A few awards were on the walls and windows on the south and west sides looked out on Arch and Broad Streets. On his desk was a framed photo of his dead wife who had started the agency with desires to be a dominate female private eye.

"Rumor has it that you wanted to see me, Mr. Goldberg?"

"I did at nine, but as usual you're late."

"There was a fire, well, and explosion in my apartment building. I could've died." She clutched her heart.

"I had thought maybe your brother was sick again. Do you have a brother, Dotty?"

"He's on death row in a state prison. Him and my dad had a flare up, a carving knife got involved. Last Thanksgiving dinner my family ever shared."

The agency's owner was sitting at his desk staring out of the window at the statute of Ben Franklin on the top of City Hall. He was the same height as Dotty but in great shape for early sixties. He wore contacts most times and cheap suits paired with clip-on ties. He finally looked at Dotty and frowned.

"Tell me about this morning, ma'am?"

"The fire? What about it?"

"Before the fire."

Dotty wanted to run. She reached into her pocket for a toothpick and couldn't find one. She wondered how many people watched her ushering a dead nun to a car.

"This morning, you mean?" she asked.

THE DRUNK DETECTIVE

"You're playing games. This morning, last night, you know what the hell I mean. When people with jobs to report to in the a.m. are sleeping. Just what do you think you were doing?"

"You've talked to Bishop Sinclair?"

"Who? You thought it best to jeopardize your job by calling me just after midnight asking about who I sleep with?"

"Who me?"

Luscious Goldberg spun in his chair and stood up. He got up close to Dotty, and clear gray eyes stared deeply at her. "Let me help jog your vodka-fogged memory since amnesia is your defense. Let's play dumb-dumb games. I don't appreciate you waking me up asking if I sleep with a blow up doll."

"Who did that?" She resisted the urge to laugh.

"You claimed to have a bet with a guy at the bar."

"Oh my. Did I tell you the name of the bar?"

"That's besides the point. What you do on your time is your business, thank the Lord, but when you involve me in your off the wall antics, I will put my foot so far up your ass, you'll cough up shoe polish."

"I was white girl wasted."

"I wouldn't know you sober. That's part of the problem. No more drinking on my clock. That's a new rule, you got that?"

"Oh, come on. I meet clients at bars. They're depressed. We drink. It wouldn't be polite for me not to drink with them."

"Dotty, there's always a pint of gin in your desk trash can and a fifth of vodka in your car's arm rest and I bet you have a flask in your left pocket right now. You're a walking speakeasy. If a client invites you to drink, give them their money back. I hope that's loud and clear.

"Goldberg does inquirers," he added. "That means employee thefts, criminal background checks, look for missing teens. No divorces. No peeking in peepholes. And we do not photograph or blackmail adulterers."

"Yes, sir."

"When my wife died, her will demanded that I keep you on staff and I don't know what she liked about you. There's nothing to like. But I am prepared to have my lawyers help me break my wife's will to toss you into the streets on your big ass. Last night's little call almost had me there. You got that?"

"Yes, sir."

"You say, 'Yes sir,' but I bet you're really thinking, 'to hell with you asshole,' aren't you?"

"No, sir."

"Then, you're dumber than I surmised. That's why you're assigned to the file room." He leaned closer. "I'm really a problem for you, Dotty. A bad nightmare. Every day I will have you in my office to piss you off forcing you to quit. Or. Please make it easy to fire you and deal with the courts to keep you out."

"Yes, sir. Sir?"

"Oh my God. What?"

Dotty stood up. "So, did I win the bet?"

"Get the hell outta my office."

She got the hell out, and found a toothpick.

THE DRUNK DETECTIVE

CHAPTER 20

En route to the file room she bumped into Naim Butler. The University of Pennsylvania Law School intern was rushing and dropped a file he was reading as he walked.

"If your head was up you would've seen me," Dotty said. "You sign that file out? I doubt it, because I'm here."

"I will when I get back." He was gathering papers from the floor. "I think I figured out whose been stealing at Century 21 department store."

"You're still working on thefts at a store with security?"

"Well management believes security is in on the thefts." Naim raised thick, bushy eyebrows eminently crafted for raising. He was in his late twenties and very athletic, with jet black hair and bright brown eyes. "How'd you even know I was looking into the matter?"

"I am in charge of files. I read them. You're wasting your time with the women. Scott Dempsey's your guy."

"So that you know, you're not supposed to be poking your nose in the files. They're confidential."

"What am I supposed to do in that room? Look at porn on my cell phone? I read yours. You ought to take that girl serious."

He blushed. "That isn't your business. Hold up, Queta's not in my personnel record."

"If all your dates were in human resources' data base, you'd be fired. Does Luscious teach you anything?" She smirked.

Naim shifted gears. "So why Scott Dempsey? He's the assistant head of security, why would he steal and risk his job? We've nailed Anita Brockingham ripping off the store five years ago, and she now works for them again."

"Newsflash, we didn't catch a soul. I caught the thieving bitch. It was just before Donna kicked the bucket and left Father Brass Balls to harass me. If you read the files and stop looking for red herrings, you'll learn Dempsey has a side job. Maybe he steals and resells the items on E-bay or in the Amazon store. He could be vying for the head of security job. In order for that to happen the head has to go."

"But how will I find out if he's selling the goods, Dotty? I can't get subpoenas, that you know."

"What the fuck? You're an investigator. Investigate. Tail him. Take photographs. Hack into his laptop from a remote location. I bet he has a broad he's cheating on the wife with in a pink Chanel suit and a new tit job, both of which he paid for, and it won't be Caitlyn Jenner."

"That has nothing to do with the theft. Mr. Goldberg says..."

THE DRUNK DETECTIVE

"Who's case is it? You or his?"

"Mine, but..."

Dotty put her arm around his shoulders. "Listen, clients pay for answers and I assure you he's spending the money on some broad. They all do. Find the girl, get the evidence, and get paid. Clients come back. Goosey Lucy's ecstatic. Your recommendation letter is marvelous. Having integrity is for pussies."

"I guess I can spy on him for a day or two. I have a new car, a Charger."

"That's all the equipment you need to track a person. Trust me, a woman has him risking his job. He'll confess to the thefts to avoid a nasty divorce."

"I hope this works."

"Guts. It's what got me where I am."

"A file clerk."

"Asshole."

"Thanks, though, Dotty. I don't know why Mr. Goldberg wants you run over by an ambulance."

"Screw him. He sleeps with blow up dolls." Dotty went on her merry way to the file room, severely proud of herself. It was like training dolphins at Sea World.

The file room was windowless, a former closet. It was filled with file cabinets, but Luscious had all the files recorded in a computer data base. Dotty was sure Donna Goldberg didn't approve of it, or the fact that Prestige Detective Agency had been using a pen name since her death. Her desk was a legendary Prestige piece with a chair that screamed in pain whenever she sat in it or swiveled in it. On top was the only black rotary phone left in America. First thing, she checked the wastebasket and found that her pint of Southern Comfort whiskey had been impounded. She took a swig of Wild Irish Rose bum wine from her pocket flask. She mixed her drink colors religiously, not doing so was for punks. Dotty was the youngest of two children of a school janitor and school secretary in rural West Chester, Pennsylvania. The secretary skipped town and took all of the savings and a younger man with her. Dotty's father hated his children afterward and beat them with the Bible as often as he could.

Daily.

Whatever her and her brother did wrong, it was fixed with advice that always began with, 'The Bible says...' Dotty couldn't do anything right, and as soon as she turned seventeen she moved out of her father's house taking her a nice memento: her father's prosthetic leg. He had lost the original one God gave him in a work related accident. In Dotty's mind, he couldn't chase after her with Bible in hand without a leg to stand on. He had her arrested and the judge forced them to therapy. Dotty went to one session alone, because her father refused to participate. She too was banned after she left with the psychiatrist's Smith-Corona electric typewriter on her way out. For this she was arrested a second time in a month, and all hope was lost.

Dotty, however, didn't imagine a fierce crime spree in her future as she wanted no parts of jail. Going to jail was a lovely deterrent for the wild teen. Her intimate knowledge of how criminals worked though gave her the foresight to become a private detective, since no police agency would hire her for her past thefts. She looked through the Yellow Pages for a detective agency that handled divorces. Her parents had been through one, and she knew how to spot the signs of a divorce lurking. Using her brand new typewriter she forged letters from three detective agencies from Miami for one reason only, they were really busy and she doubted they'd be available to confirm her employment especially since she left phony telephone numbers. Donna had hired her on the spot. When a cop Dotty was investigating for his wife figured out that she was eighteen and a high school drop out, Donna Goldberg didn't fire her. She gave her a raise. Besides, the cop's wife paid a handsome boon for the goods to settle her divorce in her favor.

Over Thanksgiving dinner Dotty's father wasn't impressed with her new job. Although, he had forgiven her for stealing the leg, he called her names and guessed that she'd fail, pissing off her big brother, Donald. Donald was carving the turkey when an argument kicked up and he started carving the old man instead, killing him and lowering Black and Decker cordless electric knife stocks. He was found guilty by reason of insanity and currently at Norristown State Hospital for the criminally insane. Dotty told people he was on death row because it sounded more dangerous and he'd likely die there. With dad dead and her brother in jail, Dotty set to move back home, but her mother reappeared and now wanted to claim the house for her and lover boy. Dotty told her to shove the house up her ass and left after she flushed her mother's dentures down the toilet. To Dotty there was nothing more exciting than divorce.

When the flask was dry, she stopped reminiscing, got off her ass, and started filing. There was a short stack of folders on her desk and she peeked in them before placing them in file cabinets. She knew Luscious had all of the good files with the things that were of interest to her locked in his office. Until noon, she went out of her mind in the lonely room and drew faces on pictures of Luscious in the desktop advertising calendar given to clients. Then she went to lunch.

Her favorite bar was Moriarty's Restaurant and Irish Pub on 11th and Walnut Streets, and that was where she was headed. Despite the rain drizzling down she didn't mind the walk. Harry's Bar was closer inside of the Marriott Residence Inn hotel, but she owed, Tommy, the bartender there. Moriarity's had great food and a cheap lunch bar menu for the downtown suits that like to get loose on their lunch breaks like Dotty.

"Hey, Dotty, how you doin'? The usual?" Bebo, the one-eye bandit, black, bartender who owned the place and only worked the lunch crowd with his pit-bull, Puffy. It was at this time he met the investors in his business. This one and the low-key numbers racket he had going on with the South Philadelphia Irishman named, Two Roses Rob, supposedly half Italian and named for the two roses that he left at his three alleged murder scenes.

"Make it a double." Dotty climbed into a stool. The pit-bull, popped his head up from the hardwood floor behind the bar, spied Dotty, yawned and went back to sleep.

Dotty fanned away the stench from Puffy's yawn as Bebo dropped a shot of Seagram's gin and a glass of Corona in front of her. "You need to put mints in the dog's food."

"I gotta stop letting him drink milk."

Dotty demolished the shot and chased it with a gulp of beer. "Hit me, Bebo."

"I can't believe you're here after last night. I was sure you was going to crash that Mercedes." He refilled the shot glass with a little extra.

"Was I here?"

"You don't remember. You danced on the bar. Security had to force you to get down. You then gave a lap dance to Two Roses Rob. That had to be scary."

THE DRUNK DETECTIVE

Dotty looked over her shoulder at Two Roses Rob who was doing a Sudoku puzzle. "Did I make a bet with him."

"What bet?"

She turned back. "You see me make a call?"

"I don't know how you could."

"Did I leave around midnight?"

"Dotty, you came after midnight."

"Do you know where I was before?"

Bebo shook his head. "You're the detective asking me all of the questions."

"This is crazy."

"Must be some shit to lose the whole night."

"I lost all of this year." She knocked back the drink and chased it. "Hit me, again."

"You missed Obama's first inauguration, too, I bet."

Dotty watched him pour. "How'd you lose your eye, anyway?"

"Dick was hard and I looked down to quick," he said as the bar's phone rang. He answered it. With a hand over the mouthpiece: "You here to meet a date named, Rodriguez?"

Dotty took the phone. "Are you following me?"

"Should I be. You are on my list. Your boss gave me a list of places to find you. All bars." The connection smelled of fire. "Can you come by the Round House?"

"As in police headquarters?"

"Yes, I have questions and concerns."

"Like?"

"Like who was out to kill Frankie Robinson. Who would try to fry him? This is definitely arson now. I need you here now, or you may be talking to someone else, and maybe at your job, a fact that I doubt you can stand after talking to your boss."

"Someone else?"

"Homicide, if he dies."

Dotty said she'd be there and hung up. "Fuck me."

"I didn't literally mean my dick poked my eye out. I mean, I'm huge, but you know."

"I got bad news, Dumb-bo."

"Oh, good. You couldn't handle a Viagra induced thirteen-inch schlong."

"Goodbye, Bebo. I have to go." She stood up.

"Payment."

"Today is on you for enduring your bad sex jokes."

Puffy, the pit-bull yawned again.

Bebo waved the fumes with the bar rag. "You got that, Dotty. Tomorrow he'll be on Altoids."

THE DRUNK DETECTIVE

CHAPTER 21

"Let me guess, now you're Miss Marple?"

Rodriguez burped and then offered Dotty a seat. His desk was make of oak with burn marks on the ends closes to him. On his desk was a poorly made Improvised Explosive Device (also known as a booby trap).

"Your kid's science fair project? And stop comparing me to fake TV detectives. These breasts are real, baby."

"No it's an explosive device used to rig the electrical socket. This is a model of the one used in your building. You know how to work it? I doubt it. By the looks of your saggy breasts you haven't worked out in ages."

"By golly, gosh darn it, heavens no, Mr. Fireman. How do you use this thing?"

"You're an ass. Basically, it's used to cross up the wires to create a spark of fire when the switch is turned on. The fire in combination with the fumes from the stove caused the explosion. Quite amateurish, although, painfully effective."

"Now you're cooking with fire," Dotty said with interest and he frowned. "Sorry, bad fire joke."

"Really, though? You're smarter than you...well, than I thought. Any who, we asked your landlord about it and he said every apartment has a light switch at the door. He said that he had all of the electrical wiring replaced less than a year ago. Either he's lying or he was stiffed by an electrician."

"Either is possible knowing Chen. He's a slumlord."

"How cute the way you describe the man that gives you a roof over your head despite your constant late rent payments."

"He told you that? Sounds libelous."

"But yeah. Just before your pal comes home, someone turned on all of the burners on the stove and blew out the flames. The dudes out for the night which is what he does for a living. By the time he gets home the fumes have permeated the place really good. He opens the door, flips the light switch." He banged his hand on the desk. "Boom."

"Jesus." Dotty jumped.

"Because he only weighed one-hundred-fifty-five pounds, he was thrown across the hall instead of being blown to smithereens. The light weight saved his life. The report of the burn unit ain't good. He's burned over fifty-percent of his body."

"I guess his career is over."

Rodriguez didn't say anything. He put a cigarette out on one of the corners of his desk.

"Why'd you want me here. I don't even know how to change the light on my bedroom lamp."

"Yeah. I wanted to ask you what kind of landlord is Chen?"

"He's a real slime-ball."

"You don't like him it sounds like."

"I didn't say that. If I hated slime-balls I'd have no friends."

"You're friends?"

"Look. I didn't say that either."

Rodriguez flipped the butt into a plastic wastebasket and Dotty panicked. She leaned over and saw the bottom of the can filled with water. "I asked about him because he was agitated when I asked had anyone been in the apartment that morning besides Frankie Robinson."

"And he said?"

"He didn't have a clue. Asked if I thought he was a weirdo that peeped out of his door's peephole at his tenants?"

"Did you tell him you did?"

"He's a lying sack of shit. You know liars in this business, he seemed to be protecting someone."

"Man, he wouldn't protect Pope Francis. You badger him like you're doing me?"

"I pushed him to the point that I wanted to take him for a ride in the squad car to a dark area on Delaware Avenue and dump him in the river. See if he could swim. I only called you here because every tenant said you've been living there before they moved in. I assumed you'd know Chen well."

"He takes my coins monthly. That's the extent of it."

"What about the two gentlemen you were with this morning?"

Dotty reached for a toothpick to mask the fact that she had flinched. So Rodriguez was that kind of arson investigator. "I guess you've talked to Lombardo?"

"Should we?"

Holy shit. She didn't know if the old bat or the cop that drilled her gave up the tapes. "I went overboard with the drinks last night," she said. "Maybe I brought two guys back with me for a menage trois. I sent them home around five."

"You're lying through your teeth. Names?"

She huffed. "You ever been white girl wasted? I mean, shit-faced."

"I've drank like a fish, but I smoke mostly."

"The whole bar knows your name, and you theirs. But you don't remember them."

"Where were you drinking?"

"Moriarty's where you called me, for some time. I don't recall before or after that."

"Then you've got a big problem."

"I do. I'm an alcoholic."

"You can't account for everything. No one knows when Frankie went out. Perhaps you and your two pals rigged the booby trap and the gas before the explosion."

"No motive."

"This isn't damn TV, Dotty. I can arrest you without motive and let a prosecutor make that part up."

"But..."

"A hooker, although, a male hooker, could find many easy ways to die. Maybe you had a tab with him." Dotty laughed. "I called another bar looking for you, and learned you hadn't been there since you had a tab." Rodriguez leaned his head to the side and squeezed his eyebrows together. "Bottom-line, if I was you I'd produce those friends."

"What makes me the fall, gal?"

THE DRUNK DETECTIVE

"First of all, you should've told me that two strangers were in the building. Maybe they tricked you to get into the apartment. Your neighbor was blown up that's worth mentioning."

"I didn't see a connection. I walked them out and locked up. What's another?"

"I don't like you at all."

"Trust me, the feeling is soooooo mutual."

"I could give two fucks, Dotty Davis." Rodriguez lit another cigarette. "So you know, it was Mrs. Lombardo that told us thee of you were on the stairs. In between stories about her rendezvous at Sugar House Casino."

"Maybe you should gamble there, but not with me 'cause I didn't try to kill the man. May I go?"

"I have a Mass to get to anyway. Let me know if you plan to leave town. You know the drill."

Dotty stood. "What kind of Mass takes place on Monday?"

"It's a memorial service. The nun, Sister Tudor, principal of my daughter's school died sometime last night. They found her this morning at the pew unresponsive. She was announced dead. You don't look good. You OK?"

Dotty coughed and shot the toothpick right into the wastebasket with the wet butts. "Fine. I almost swallowed that. What did you say the Sister's name was again?"

"Sister Anne Tudor."

"She was my daughter's teacher many moons ago. And to think we had nothing in common. Sure you're OK?"

"I may go back to smoking again, you make it seem so palatable." She left out.

* * *

"Dotty come with me. New rule. I know you love them," said Luscious Goldberg. "No more two-hour lunches."

Jack had sent her right into the office with one of his classic grins. Dotty said, "I had to see a man about a fire."

"You really should watch your words."

"Man?"

"Fire. F. I. R. E. Fire." He sounded like a Spelling Bee contestant.

She stopped at Jack's desk. He was still reading the same paper. What an idiot, she thought.

"Naim Butler around?"

"He left a while ago with a camera around his neck. Luscious gave you hell, huh? Tell me all of the details." He closed the newspaper, leaned back in his chair and cupped his hands behind his head.

"I hope he has a good flash. A young black man with a criminal history looking to be a private investigator. He reminds me of myself."

"You're an old bag. And white. Hardly a good comparison. Besides, he's a vibrant ivy-league law student that was recruited to a firm in New York. They're paying for his law school. He's nothing like you."

"You can hate on me, I'm still the same old G."

"Rapping doesn't make you like him. Oh, this came for you by courier." He held up an envelope.

Dotty didn't take it. "Any windows?"

"Nope."

"My ex-husband's penmanship? I hope ex."

"How the hell I know?"

"Jackie Ottaman serves subpoenas in plain clothes, but she's a county sheriff. Was she a big rectangular gal with a dumb face?"

"You're a big rectangular gal with a dumb face."

She took it. The envelope was heavy cream stock, addressed in fine calligraphy. "'Ms. Dorothy Davis,'" she read aloud.

"Obviously, they don't know you."

She opened it.

{Dear Ms. Davis,

If I am not intruding on prior plans, your presence this evening at six o'clock with be advantageous for you and I.

Very truly yours,

Bernard Sinclair

Papal Nuncio}

A card with a Society Hill address engraved on it was paper-clipped to the letter, along with a new Ben Franklin bill.

"FBI, I hope?" Jack inquired.

"Religious mail." She refolded everything and stuffed it all into in her pocket.

He opened his newspaper. "It's a bit late for that."

CHAPTER 22

"Get lost."

"You shouldn't talk to your partner in crime like that," Dotty said.

"Ex-partner. I got the boot, not you, because of a clause in a will. Now, I'm booting you. Get lost."

Patrick Swayze worked at a Wells Fargo as an assistant manager in Two Penn Center. He had a chiseled face, small frame and dominate black eyebrows like former president Lincoln, which he tried to soften with pastel shirts and Windsor knots in his ties. It was five o'clock on the dot and he was stuffing his briefcase to get out of the office.

"You have a fine job. The boot didn't hurt you one bit," Dotty said.

"You're right. Just my wife and daughter and the freedom I had as a detective. Now I'm in the rat race with these people. I hate you."

"Come on, Swayze."

THE DRUNK DETECTIVE

"Get lost, Dotty."

"Hell it was a sweet case. All you had to do was like I told you and sell the photos to the husband. You weren't supposed to tell Luscious a thing."

"You could've taken the fall since you couldn't be fired. They wanted to have me arrested."

"Well they didn't so what's the problem?" They were walking out of the bank.

Outside, in front of the Clothes Pin Statute, Swayze said, "I was out of work for a year because no one believed I was named Patrick-Fucking-Swayze. Can you imagine that on a resume, if you're not the Dirty Dancing star. My wife divorced me and took my little girl to Florida. I haven't seen either of them in years."

Dotty leaned an elbow on the wall of which on the other side had a twelve feet drop leading to the subway. "Kids cost to damn much, and they turn out to be problems in their teens. Be glad that you're free. I am."

When she came to, she was on her back on the ground being ignored by passerby. Swayze now leaned on the wall and kissed his knuckles.

"What brought you here, Dotty?"

"You've been in the gym, I see." She sat up, tasting blood. "You didn't used to hit me that way. I owe you."

"You weren't as fat and slow either. Get the hell up to, but know I'll knock you back down."

"I believe I have crosshairs on my back."

"I will send the assassin a bonus check."

"I'm not joking."

"Neither am I. There's plenty of money in that bank."

"You hear about the male prostitute that was blown up this morning?"

"Gas explosion? I have."

"Welp, it wasn't an accident."

"OMG, you blew up a man-whore?"

"No, what the hell do I look like?"

"I don't know, but you looked like a pile of dog shit on the ground a second ago."

"It happened in my building. Someone broke in, messed with the light switch, and filled the place with gas before heading out."

"Smart. What was he into besides giving someone's wife pleasure and why're you involved?"

"He was giving more than wives pleasure and obviously pain." Dotty told him the story, beginning with Frankie Robinson's call and finishing with the arson investigator's discovery. She left out the small detail about the staged photos she had created.

"You mean the Sister Tudor the news reported being found by the alter boy at the pew counting Hail Mary's at the Our Lady of the Rosary church this morning?" Swayze asked.

"Thanks to me and a creep, Lynch."

"Tell me more."

"The explosion was for the doll, ain't that the obvious? Lynch thought we were in my apartment and tried to off me and clean up any evidence to link the Church to yet another sex scandal. Luckily, I went back to my place and to bed."

"Missing something. The bishop doesn't need to kill you. He's quite capable of handling scandals."

Dotty sucked her lip to stop the bleeding. "You're a damn fool. This diocese can't take another incident. He'd do anything to keep this quiet, even try to kill me."

"Then you should feel fortunate. Justice missed you by a hair. You've wronged more than ten prostitutes ever could and needed to pay up."

"Screw you. The thing is, I was summoned to the rectory to see the bishop in an hour. Maybe he has a bullet with Dotty written on it."

"Don't go."

"I have to. Could be a business deal."

"You're going to scam the Church. You must have pictures. You're going straight to hell, do not pass GO."

"Just thirty of them. I even took pics of Lynch and his car with the dead nun in the front seat before they pulled off. Oh, and I recorded the pull off until the Caddy turned the corner. They have money, why shouldn't I get some."

"Ask Frankie. He got some money, now look at him."

"I will, but for now I E-mailed you photos to a Dropbox account, but you can't access them unless I am dead. Young kid, Naim Butler, at the agency is going to give you the info if I don't contact you by ten p.m. Here's his number." She handed him a slip of paper with a number written on it.

"I'm not doing that. Fuck you, Dotty."

"Come on, Swayze. I figured your heart was as big as your ass."

He pushed her down. She bounced back up.

"You're pretty strong."

"Been working out. I told you that."

"Look you're the only friend I've got."

"To hell I am. I'm not your friend."

"Come on. I'll call you by ten from my home phone only. Thank God they killed the fire before it hit my place."

"You're one lucky whore. Gin flames aren't easy to put out."

Dotty left, blotting her lip with a handkerchief. She drove towards the rectory with one hand on the steering wheel and the other trying to stop the bleeding, but she could tell it was beginning to swell. She took Market Street right down passing the Gallery Mall and the United States Courthouse. The Society Hill neighborhood was at the end of Market Street (an eight minute drive from the bank), and the Church was right on Fifth and Chestnut Streets, adjacent to the first US Capital.

Her lip stopped bleeding. Before someone answered the door she looked at her face in a compact mirror and stuffed the handkerchief in her pocket.

"Dotty Davis."

Perched in the opened doorway, Lynch looked even more sinister than he did this morning at Frankie Robinson's apartment. He had on the same coat buttoned to the top and his bald head and a little stubble on it in the light.

Dotty's eyes had widened. "I wasn't expecting to see you."

"My Lord is expecting you."

"People know my whereabouts."

"Good for them. Or not." He stepped aside.

THE DRUNK DETECTIVE

Dotty entered the foyer hung with raspberry-colored drapes and followed Lynch down a marble lined hall that looked fresh. At the end Lynch knocked on a door, and a voice invited them inside.

The bishop was a midget of a man with a pouch above his waist mirroring a basketball, with jet-black hair parted in the middle and brushed to each side falling to the white shackle of his clerical collar. He rose from behind a cherry-wood desk, wearing a black cassock that swept the floor and he looked like a wizard in a Harry Potter production on the Avenue of the Arts. The cavernous room was square and smelled of the cheap leather that bound the books on the shelves. A large crucifix made of pearl hung on the wall behind the desk. Lynch and Dotty walked in and the bishop closed the door behind them.

"Thanks for joining us, Ms. Davis," said the bishop. "Take a seat."

"It was the money." She settled into a leather chair that gripped her ass like a hand in a soft glove.

"Were you in an accident?"

"Just my lip."

The bishop took a seat at the desk with his back to the crucifix.

"I wanted to thank you in person for doing such a fine job this morning," he said. "The Church doesn't have to many friends right now. Do you happen to be Catholic?"

"Nope. Too much kneeling. Same reason I couldn't keep my husband."

The bishop nodded as if he understood. "I am quite disturbed by Sister Tudor's indiscretion. I hoped she would be canonized soon and help revive the diocese."

"I guess she found other ways to be revived herself."

He smiled. "I am destined for cardinal. His Holiness practically gave me the red hat during his visit here last year for the Meeting of the Families Celebration. Of course, it's not official, yet."

"You've made plane reservations to Rome and all I bet."

"Don't interrupt His Eminence."

"It's OK, Lynch. If I lost my patience I wouldn't be in this position."

Dotty said, "Your leading lady checking in and then out in a prostitutes bed wouldn't work so good for your image in Rome, I'm sure. Of course, that's why you tried to blow me into tiny pieces."

"How so?"

"The lynch mob director here didn't know that I lived above Frankie. He rigged his apartment to blow my pretty face off, only it blew off Frankie's work equipment."

"What is she talking about?"

"The gigolo's apartment caught fire this morning," Lynch said. "I saw it on the news, that's how I know about it."

"You weren't responsible?"

"Oh my God," Dotty said. "Pardon my French, Father."

"That building is a death trap, Your Excellency. A fire could have easily started there."

"Cops found an IED that started it." Dotty folded her arms, causing the leather to fart. "I have pictures. Lots of them. They're with a friend as we speak. You know the drill."

"You looking to extort the Church?"

"I'm not dressed to be an extortionist. Let's just call it blackmail."

On a serving cart was a silver tray containing two long-stemmed glasses and a cut-crystal decanter half-filled with crimson-colored liquid. The bishop removed the stopper and poured a glass for Dotty and himself.

"We should drink. This post allows me two vices: a little red wine and I smoke a Cuban cigar a day."

"And what are we celebrating, Your Excellency?"

Dotty resisted the urge to touch either glass.

"Your new job as chief of diocesan security. The pay is as handsome as you and the hours are easy."

Dotty smiled and rubbed her hands together. "Am I now Lynch's boss?"

"Dotty please with the dumb questions," said Lynch.

"Lynch works directly for me. The chief of security works without supervision and has an office downtown at the diocese headquarters."

"And in return I develop a case of amnesia?"

"And pass along all relevant material to me, naturally." The bishop sipped from his glass.

Dotty lifted hers then. "What's to stop Lynch from polishing me off after that?"

"Neither Lynch or I had anything to do with that fire. You have a dim view of religion."

"Come on. People getting burned at the stake and nailed to the cross, what'd you expect." She gulped down half her wine. It wasn't that good.

"Are you familiar with the bible, Davis?"

"I knew my dad's up, close and personal. He beat me with it."

"Then you know how important your secrecy is. Do you accept the position?"

"I don't really want to be cooped up in an office. I like my current job. Tell you what: put me on retainer, for a few grand per month to do discreet inquirers, and I keep the pictures for a lifetime. Think of it as a lifetime appointment."

"Not a chance. The pictures are apart of the deal no matter how you slice it."

"Well, you're shit out of luck. 'Scuse my Flen--French." The room was beginning to close and the air thickened. She could barely take a deep breath.

"Your Excellency?"

"Do nothing yet, Lynch."

Dotty's grin spilled all over her face. She dumped the balance of her wine chasing the intoxicating feeling that it gave her. "Don't feel bad Lynch. I know you're not the first person the bishop ordered around." Her vision was blurring and she began to think there was a point to the theory about not mixing the grape with the grain.

"Are you all right, Davis? I fear my company is putting you to sleep."

Dotty could no longer see the bishop or the crucifix behind him. They were both shadows. She leaned over to return her glass to the tray and kept going, to the floor.

THE DRUNK DETECTIVE

She thought, dammit, I bet this means no job either.

MARY JEAN CURRY

CHAPTER 23

She awoke feeling no different than she did every other morning, with her head pounding and a tongue blown up the size of a Boeing seven-forty-seven. Her eyes were glued shut with crust.

She rubbed them, pried them open, and thought she had lost her sight. A street lamp beamed on her and she shifted forcing a cheap bottle of wine to fall to the floor of the judge's luxury car. Something in three jackets and a man's fedora was on the floor prying off her shoes.

"What are you doing?"

A dirty face looked up at her. An old fashioned face, possibly female, slim nostrils, blood shot eyes, and no more than two teeth in a pink hole of a mouth. Dotty smelled wine. Or maybe whiskey.

"I assumed you were here because you were dead," said the monster.

"I'm not."

THE DRUNK DETECTIVE

"Are you certain? I seen dead rats get up and scurry away because no one told them."

"Retard. Get off my damn feet."

"Dead people don't need shoes. I don't know why people waste money burying dead people in them."

"Old man, you don't either."

He moved back. "You're parked in a cemetary. No need to be here if you're alive."

"What?" Dotty popped up and looked around at all of the headstones.

"Yes. Greenmount Cemetary."

"Jesus. You sure this ain't the Marriot Hotel."

He cackled. It sounded like ice being chopped in a blender. "Now that I think about, maybe it is. This here is a Philadelphia cheese steak. Sorry no fries." He pulled a dead mouse from a jacket and dangled it by its tail.

"You eat mice?"

"You can have half for the shoes."

{Where's my gun,} Dotty thought. {Maybe the glove box.} She popped it open and the man threw his hand up and caught a fifth of vodka. He unscrewed the cap and took a huge swig. Dotty reached for the other bottle and took a long pull. As she let the liquor warm her belly, she pondered about Patrick Swayze. He was supposed to call the cops at ten.

"Give me my lucky ascot asshole."

"I didn't take no ascot. Do I look like I wear fuckin' ascots?"

She turned on the car and looked at the clock. It was 10:16. "Holy macro."

"I have to go."

"Leave me the rest of the bottle."

"Get lost." She slammed the door shut and swung the car out onto Front Street. She drove through the Hunting Park section of North Philadelphia hoping not to be carjacked in the crime ridden area. The area was home to turf wars, prostitution, and the drug trade. Even Lynch treaded lightly after dropping her off so far from downtown.

Her time with the bishop was still a blur. Whatever the bishop had slipped her had to have been clear and in her glass before he handed it to her. Surely a premeditated attempt to show her who was in charge. Why didn't he just kill her? Certainly, Lynch could handle that. Whatever the drug was it was good, because her memory was back and she even knew where she was the night before. As luck would have it, she had had a marvelous night.

She got onto the busy, and heavy populated Broad Street, and called Swayze from her cell phone.

"Hello?"

"Patrick. Dotty."

"Get out of my life."

"Stop the jokes, OK. Did you send the photos to the cops, yet?"

"Huh? Photos? What are you talking about?"

"The ones I E-mailed for you, idiot."

"Oh, no, I didn't."

"You're an ass. Why not?"

"Why not what?"

"If you didn't hear from me you was supposed to send them off."

THE DRUNK DETECTIVE

"OK, I didn't. Move on."

"What's the point in using you if you're not going to do your part?"

"You're right. Did you pay me? Did you get any money out of the Church?"

"I got drugged."

"What's new?"

"Man, they slipped me something. Knocked me out and I awoke in a cemetary with a bum trying to take my penny loafers."

"Only a bum would want them."

"Look, Swayze, if you don't hear from me in twenty-four hours, please get the pics to a cop named, Rodriguez. He's an arson investigator."

"OK, when do I get my money?"

"Listen, if you have to send the pics I'll be dead."

"Then I'll be a winner." He hung up.

Dotty hung up and imagined being confronted by Chen as soon as she walked into the apartment building about his cut of {her} money. Her landlord wanted money. Her pal, Patrick, also wanted money. Neither of them realized, she wanted to squeeze money out of someone just as bad. The money from the he-bitch was chump change and Chen had already put a dent in it. She hoped Chen hadn't reported her little tampering with a crime scene to the police. She dialed the massage parlor and Chen's home number and both rang nine-thousand times without an answer.

Chen had never went anywhere. He had his groceries delivered and was a frequent online shopper. Where the hell could he be?

"The precinct. Dammit." Dotty hurried around a SEPTA bus and spun the Benz's wheels just over sixty mph.

Chen didn't own a car and hated to pay for taxis. He surmised he'd be kidnapped by an UBER driver and thought it was the riskiest business created since prostitution. Dotty made a left onto Vine Street and hoped she'd intercept Chen walking to the cop house. She knew his distinct walk and knew she'd see it a mile away. Dotty thought she saw him posted up at a corner, but it turned out to be an inflatable doll that some idiot had leaned on one of the last phone booths left in the city.

The massage parlor was pitched black, with the CLOSED sign in the window over Kim Kardasian's boobs. Dotty paralleled into the space where Lynch's vehicle had been earlier and slid into the apartment's foyer. The security buzzer hadn't worked since Clinton's first term.

Dotty knocked on Chen's door and waited.

"You're probably looking at me through the peephole, you fucker. Open up," she said, knocked again, and then turned the knob.

She walked right on into the apartment. It was neat with the kind of flare made for an apartment in Trump Tower. It was obvious how he spent his money collecting poor people's rent. "Pompous bastard," she said and helped herself to a Mike's Hard Lemonade in a well appointed kitchen.

She walked around swishing the cooler in her mouth to get rid of the poisoned wine taste.

No Chen.

She helped herself to a Swarovski crystal shot glass before heading to the door. She had no idea where Chen was, but it wasn't like him to call or go to the police, period; especially,

THE DRUNK DETECTIVE

when the money came if he didn't. Free money was Chen's first wish if asked by a genie.

Brooding if he might be at Frankie Robinson's place assessing the damage, or creating more, for insurance policy purposes, Dotty hopped off of a mohair sofa, locked up (there were thieves in the building), and bound the stairs to Frankie's apartment. The hallway smelled of smoke and stale water drying.

Chen wasn't there, either. The door to the burnt apartment was boarded by crime scene tape. She doubted that he was in there.

She went up to her floor, hoping Chen hadn't used his key and was waiting in her apartment. The key really was pointless considering Adam the fireman and his chop for gigolos.

Dotty's first thought was that she needed to get her place in order. She needed to throw everything away and start over from scratch. The living room sofa was faux leather which was peeling and missing leather exposing cotton. A travesty. Thanks to the wine, the spiritual wine, her memory was slowly resurfacing. Why was her glove box in such disarray that the vodka bottle popped right out when she opened it? The bum had no reason to leave it there.

Lynch did.

She wondered what had he learned about her from being in there, besides she had liquor, which wasn't so bad since the bishop drank wine and smoked cigars.

Dotty walked towards her bedroom anticipating a shower. The door was shut, something that she never did. {Where's my gun?} Having no idea, she grabbed a small bat kept on her mantle by the front door in case she had to bludgeon a robber to death. She eased open her bedroom door and then barged in. Inside the door she tripped, lost her balance, did a ungraceful pirouette, and slammed onto the bed. Luckily. Finally, God was on her side. She bounced up, flicked on the light, and looked at Chen. Chen was what had tripped her.

The landlord was on his back, spread eagle, and undoubtedly dead. A Versace ascot was wrapped into a Windsor knot around his neck.

"Now, Chen, how'd you get my lucky ascot around your throat?"

CHAPTER 24

"Evening, Mrs. Lombardo," Dotty said.

The dame was in nursing scrubs and a leather bomber. She paused before descending the stairs, found her glasses out of her pocket, and peered through them at Dotty. "I thought that was your stuffy voice. You sound awful." She knew how to throw shade and be totally oblivious to it. "Who's that with you, hun?"

"Just a pal, ma'am." She leaned harder into Chen's soggy frame to stop him from forming a pile of poop on the old runner.

"Looks like Chen to me," she said. "You better get the stench of smoke outta my place, Chen. Don't tilt your head at me, mister China man."

Dotty laughed. She said, "He's a little choked up from smoke inhalation. You know he's as old as you. I'm taking him for a drive to get some fresh air."

"Yeah, yeah. You had him up there drinking, I bet. The whole building knows what you're into, Detective Dotty."

"Don't you have to get to work, ma'am?"

"Pardon me. I know that. I was wiping asses at that nursing home before you were born."

"Point taken. Good night, Mrs. Lombardo."

"Just a tragedy what happened to that young man, Frankie. I mean, he turned a few tricks, but that was no reason to blow him up. Don't look at me like that, Chen. The whole building knows you're a pimp. He tricks and gives you money. You sly, China man."

"Right. Just horrible." Dotty's shoulder was going to sleep and cramping. "Well, good night."

"Did your other friend get home OK earlier?"

"Absolutely. She needed rest and is really resting in peace now."

"Hell, Chen doesn't look much better. You gotta stop drinking with light weights. Apparently, they can't tolerate the white lightening like you."

"I guess, you're right. Good night, Mrs. Lombardo."

"Don't forget the smell of smoke."

"He won't, ma'am."

She moved past them and made her way down. The street door locked behind her, then Dotty lifted Chen as if he was a bride and carried him to the first floor. The landlord weighed as much as a jockey, much less than Sister Tudor. She rushed because she couldn't bump into any other residents of the building. Mrs. Lombardo was a non-factor. No jury would believe her word. Dotty thought about waiting until four a.m. because apparently that was the perfect time to move a dead body. At the rate she was going, she'd have the art of moving corpses down to give a TED talk.

At the bottom, she gently sat Chen on the floor not to cause post-mortem marks. She remembered Lynch's stellar guidance, fishing into Chen's pocket for his keys. She opened the door to his lair, and inside laid Chen on his sofa and grabbed a magazine from a coffee table. She placed the news rag on Chen's chest opened to the infamous page six and crossed his arms on his stomach. With regret, she took the earlier stolen Swarovski thingy from her pocket and put it back in its place. Someone knocked on the door.

"Mr. Lee Chen? Lee Chen?"

Dotty froze like a seasoned cat burglar. The voice calling out for Chen belonged to arson investigator, Rodriguez.

"Are you home, sir? Just a few questions." He knocked some more forcing Dotty to jump. Her nerves were shot, but she remained cool.

She looked for the nearest window and past the body splayed out on the sofa unresponsive. She wanted to set off an IED to blow the door right into Rodriguez to knock him out, so that she could escape. The doorknob began to turn. She couldn't remember if she had locked the door before she put the landlord in the place he'd be found and pronounced dead.

With luck, the knob stopped turning. Someone jiggled it, though. Then there was silence, and Dotty needed Bourbon. Or maybe, vodka. Perhaps another Mikes Hard Lemonade from the landlord. She became nostalgic for the stink breath dog at Moriarty's. She prayed the cop wasn't looking for a spare key or a way to break in.

Then she heard footsteps fading away before they began to climb the stairs.

Dotty waited a second before she tiptoed over to the door and put an eye to the peephole in the door. The foyer was empty. Quickly she opened the door slipped out, and into the vestibule. Rodriguez started back downstairs. She put her cell phone to her ear, and said, "You know I really hate you. I am home now, and I am hanging up before my husband hears me," as she met Rodriguez in the foyer.

The arson investigator had a cigarette dangling from his mouth. "Our neighbors are complaining to Chen about the smell of smoke. Mrs. Lombardo, in fact, you remember her."

Ash leaked onto the floor. "I have some questions for Chen, like what time did Frankie Robinson usually get in. Or do you know?"

"Times varied. He didn't have a traditional 9-5 or set hours of operation from his lovely home-based business, you know?"

"Don't be an ass. That's why I asked."

"Look, I wasn't sleeping with him, so our times didn't have to synchronize."

"That's my issue. Since no one knows his hours, how'd the person that set up the explosion know when it'll be safe to get into the apartment?"

"Tough question, but maybe the perp is a woman and set a fake appointment at a hotel to be sure he wasn't home. Have you checked his credit cards and cell phone records."

"He's not dead, yet, so no. Do you mind if we go to your place to chat some more?"

"Can it be later? I have a date."

"No. I could just go up. Perhaps, you forgot your door was busted through."

"I forgot."

"Another blackout, huh?"

"Nope. Not at all. Just been busy. Work stuff."

"Really. In the file room. Don't look shocked, I know you're a bona fide file clerk. We can chat here. Any idea about who you brought into the building last night?"

"Been working on it. Got a date at the same bar tonight to try to get some answers for you."

"Really. I hope you can get me what I need. Listen, I'm going to let you go to your date to get the answers that I need."

"Perfect. Maybe they need you at HQ. You should get going."

"News to me." Ash fell on his blazer and he didn't bother to brush it off. "He might make it."

"He who?"

"Frankie Robinson. Docs say he's breathing on his own. Third degree burns may kill his career if he comes out of the coma, though."

"That's a good thing. I hope he recovers."

"Me too, or this turns into a murder case. I looked through the hole in your apartment door."

Christ. "OK. Hopefully, you didn't violate my Fourth Amendment right."

"You live in a sty for animals, the explosion or fireman?"

"I can't blame anyone. Just have been busy working on cases and hadn't had time to clean up."

"Oh, OK." He turned and opened the door. He paused. "Hey where's your ascot?"

"Ascot?"

"Yes, the one you had on at my office right around your neck."

"Neck?"

"I was impressed by the ascot. Women like you don't usually wear them."

"Oh." Dotty got her feelings back. "Good night, sir."

"Yup. Good night. And remember, you're still on my list."

When Rodriguez left Dotty went back to her apartment and drowned the last drops from a vodka bottle, before splashing water on her face.

Two scenarios. Either Chen had caught Lynch tearing up her apartment looking for the pictures and got himself choked for it, or it happened when Lynch came in search for it and discovered Chen already in her apartment snooping around. It didn't matter to Dotty. She liked Chen despite their problems about her rent always being late. She'd keep his camera as a memento. She worked the camera to see if it was any good after being smashed, as she dialed Patrick Swayze at his condo.

"Dotty, please, get out of my life."

"The stakes have been raised. The pictures are quite important now."

"You get my cut yet?"

"No. Not yet for crying out loud. I'm checking on my insurance policy. Things are getting out of control."

"That's just your weight."

"C'mon, Swayze."

"Don't get your panties in a snare. The pictures are safe and sound."

THE DRUNK DETECTIVE

"Thanks, best bud."

"I'm not your bud, you ass. I can't get my coins if I don't keep my end of the bargain, dummy." He hung up.

Oddly, Dotty felt like shit. If that was even possible in her life of drunken debauchery. Someone--maybe her--would have major problems when Chen was found dead. Landlords weren't on anyone's Christmas list, especially immigrants that ran massage parlors. The list of suspects ranged from chronic late rent payers (Dotty included), tenants that wanted the smell of smoke removed from the place (Dotty included), and the whole diocese. Which, under close scrutiny, may be right on the money. Mrs. Lombardo had seen Dotty with two dead bodies, but she was no prosecutor's star witness. All Dotty had to do was keep her crimes to herself. She doubted Lynch would rat her out. Or Bishop Sinclair. One fact remained simple: Lynch didn't get the film or photos of his beloved Sister Tudor, so Dotty was a lot more deadly to the Church if she was dead than alive.

Somewhat relieved, Dotty looked through her apartment, and wanted to make a fraudulent claim with FEMA to help get it cleaned up, so that she could find her gun. It was a cute, little Walther PK380 semi-automatic eight shot number that she used once to ward off a crazy husband that chased her after throwing hot beans in his face. It was then he decided she wasn't worth the trouble and he split with their daughter. Out of love for them, Dotty let them both go away and never looked for them. Now with her front door a wreck she wanted the gun close by, especially since her landlord wouldn't be buying a new door. She couldn't find it, however.

Realizing suddenly that she hadn't taken Mrs. Lombardo's advice and was drinking without out eating, she scooted to the refrigerator looking for food that wasn't in the form of liquid. She came up with a half of a cheese steak, popped it into the microwave and then drowned it in cheap squeeze cheese and ketchup before swallowing it. She was amazed at how good a two-day old cheese steak tasted.

Pushing unfolded clean laundry from one side of the sofa to another, she plopped down and decided to catch reruns of Forensic Files, the source for her arsenal of investigative tactics. To her dismay the back of the TV was removed. {You bitch," she thought of Lynch or Chen. Her need for a TV and door made her think of Frankie Robinson. His call was starting to cost her far more than previously thought. She decided to get to bed early, taking her mini-bat with her just in case Lynch returned.

The telephone pulled her out of a dream; she was at Liquor Palace, a hotel that poured liquor out of the faucets instead of water.

"Whoever you are, you'd better hang up right now, or I'll find out where you live and communicate with ISIS from your home computer, calling the FBI from your home phone to report you before I slip out."

"Amazing, you're so chipper." The caller cleared his throat. "Dotty we need to talk."

"Not this time. Who the hell are you?"

"This is Scott Sinclair."

"Who the hell is Scott Sinclair?"

"Bishop Sinclair, Dotty. Tell me you drink so much that you don't recall."

She perked up and looked at her Mickey Mouse watch. {You son of a bitch," she thought. "It's after midnight." She groaned.

THE DRUNK DETECTIVE

"Thank you. It's a fresh new day. New horizons brewing. Can you meet me at Our Lady Of the Rosary rectory at noon."

"And let you slip me another bad batch of the Church's sacred wine?"

"I am deeply sorry about that. If you'll meet me for lunch, I'll show you how much."

"I would never eat or drink in your company. No way, Jose."

"OK, fine. Just meet me, because I accept the terms of your job proposal. We should discuss this in detail over food and wine."

"No food. I'll be there, and I'll be bringing my own bottle of wine."

CHAPTER 25

Our Lady of the Rosary was a compound with a church, rectory, and a K-12 school in Center City's Society Hill area. It covered an entire city block steps away from the Constitution Center and drew visits from sitting US Presidents. Dotty parked, dashed inside the church and was enveloped by a vaulted echoing interior with three sections of pew with navy-blue-colored runners in the aisles between. At the feet of a twelve-foot crucifix with a porcelain Jesus, a teenaged boy dressed in a white robe was busy lighting candles.

"Hey, young man." The words assaulted every wall.

The boy continued to light candles.

"What's your name, pal?"

"Jonathan Gotti."

"Bullshit."

"That's what everyone says. You shouldn't use curse words, and especially not in the Church."

THE DRUNK DETECTIVE

"My apologies. What do I owe five Hail Mary's, Jon Gotti?"

"I don't know."

"Where's your boss?"

Gotti nodded towards Jesus.

"The one one on earth, Bishop Sinclair?"

"I think the rectory."

"OK, thanks. You're awfully good with the lighter. You smoke?"

"No, ma'am."

"Drink?"

"No, ma'am."

"Curse?"

"No, ma'am!"

"Wow, you must live in a home with a single mom. You need an old man."

The boy pointed out a miniature version of the cathedral surrounded by rosebushes. Dotty left Gotti and pushed a button by the rectory's front door. When no one answered on the second buzz, she tried the knob. Maybe the bishop was asleep. She'd love to get photos of him in the buff, for blackmail purposes.

After twenty minutes, Dotty used her cell phone to call Bishop Sinclair. It rang several times.

"This is Bishop Sinclair."

"I'm on the steps, Your Bishopness," Dotty said. "Where the fuck you been the last half hour?"

"...can't come to the phone right now..."

{Bullshit. This is going to be added to the bill mister.} On her way out, she asked Gotti to relay a message, "Tell the bishop that I was here and he can reach me at home."

"OK."

"You seen him today, kid?"

"As a matter of fact, no."

"Interesting. OK. have a nice day."

* * *

During the drive home, Dotty had quite the time seeking puddles with pedestrians standing or walking nearby and ran the fancy car through them. Whenever she splashed one with dirty water, she celebrated with a gulp from her flask. At a bus stop she scored three senior citizens, a FED-EX driver, and a blind man with a seeing eye dog, and drank all of the contents left in the flask. Little awards. If she had quit her job for nothing, she'd send the pictures to the Associated Press and help Bishop Sinclair say goodbye to any ascension with the Church.

Nearing her apartment, Dotty received a call from the arson investigator.

"I need you to meet me over at U of Penn hospital ASAP. Frankie's up and talking about nothing. He refuses to divulge who tried to blow him up to anyone but you."

"I'm not a cop. I can't help him. And I hate lawyers, so, I know none. Unless I need help."

"Well you must have a way with men, because he wants to see you now, and so does his brother."

"Is that right? I do have a way with men." She was looking in her rearview mirror blushing.

"Get your ass over here." He hung up.

THE DRUNK DETECTIVE

Twenty minutes later Dotty walked onto Frankie's hospital room floor and found Rodriguez smoking a cigarette.

"That has to be illegal and unhealthy for patients," she said without preamble.

He flicked ashes onto the floor.

"Fuck you."

"Pardon me?" A mean faced orderly stopped and glared at Dotty.

"Talking to the cop." She stood with her back against the wall. "Why am I here?"

"Because you have many enemies for seventy and this is one."

"I'm fifty-six. Don't push your luck, Hun."

"No shit. Jesus life has been rough on you. All that time in the file room."

"Man, please. You're far from Tom Cruise."

"Back to the point, the man here says fuck you. Why?"

"No idea."

"Where were you last night?"

"Paddy's Old City Pub on Second and Race from happy hour to nine."

"You could've left there and rigged the switch. Where else?"

"Moriarty's Bar from nine-ten until eleven. Some dude pumped me full of drinks."

"I find that hard to believe; you're not pretty enough. Anyone else would remember you? A bartender?"

"Both should. I was pretty shit-faced."

"You're shit faced now and reek of terrible, cheap liquor."

"That's fine. But that's where I was. Why are we doing this in a hospital hallway?"

"Because I want to. What about the two guys Mrs. Lombardo saw you with this morning?"

Dotty suddenly wanted to do the unthinkable: to tell the truth. At this point she was guilty of withholding evidence, the kind of charge that wasn't a big deal. Maybe there was a law about improper disposal of a nun; but she could beat that too. A bishop had ordered her to bring the woman who died naturally home. On the flip side, the fact that Lynch had strangled Chen while tearing up her place convinced her the photos were worth their weight.

"Can't recall," she said.

"I don't get it. Why not?"

"Look, I forgot."

"Problem is yesterday you knew nothing and now you know all of your places and times, but no idea about who you brought home. Your alibis."

"I didn't rig the man's apartment to blow him up. No motive to and I would have messed up my own lovely home."

He chuckled. "You know I believe you. But something is off here."

"That's your job to get it on. So, is Frankie going to awake or what?"

"Yes, but who knows when he will be able to talk."

"You bitch." Dotty buttoned her coat. "I knew he wasn't up asking for me. I'm out of here, if you don't mind."

"I don't, but I'll be looking into these alibis. As..."

THE DRUNK DETECTIVE

"I'm still on your list."

"You got it. Before you go," the arson investigator said, signaling for a tall, handsome man to join them. "Dotty meet Frankie's brother, Hank Robinson."

"You can call me Hankie, ma'am."

She held out her hand and he grabbed it. She did a curtsy, and said, "You are a tall glass of chocolate milk, Hankie Pankie."

"What was that?"

"I digress."

"OK, I'd like to talk to you. Without the arson investigator, I mean."

Dotty had already been eyeing Hank—couldn't help it—as he stood outside of Frankie's hospital room, but right in her line of sight. He was about Dotty's height, lean in a pink Polo Ralph Lauren polo shirt, blue jeans, and Timberland boots. His features were refreshing and smooth like Frankie's, but they had to have one different parent. He looked more like twenty-five than forty-five. They retreated to the end of the hallway and he smiled at her.

"Thanks for saving my brother."

"No problem," she said. "I didn't actually save him from death as I was dead as this floor when the explosion occurred, but I rescued him from something much bigger that he needs to wake up and tell you about."

"That makes sense. He's always been known to get into trouble. I'm the good son. I haven't talked to him since we were little. Our parents gave up on him long ago. They're strict Evangelicals."

"What a shame."

"Our lives went on without him when he filmed himself masterbating and posted it on PornHub, and a member of the church found it and told the whole congregation. Some people watched the vid. When I saw him on the news, though, I was compelled to come here to help him."

"The cop lied and told him that he was conscious, son of a bitch."

"Whoa, ma'am. The language."

"I'm grown."

"A woman shouldn't talk that way." He put a hand on her shoulder and she dithered. "I'm working on a doctorate degree at U Penn, so I'd appreciate if you stayed in touch just in case he awakens. Maybe we can do lunch. I owe you for Frankie."

"Like a date?"

"Probably," he said and smiled. "Whatever floats your boat, ma'am."

"Dotty. You can call me, Dotty."

"Ms. Dotty if I'm nasty."

She covered her mouth and chuckled. "I guess you're not as born again as your parents?"

"I am. Just super flirty. But I have to go. When and if he awakens call me and I will do the same." He handed her business card with a name and number printed on it, but no profession.

"No problemmo," she said. "I am just going to tuck this into my bar, I mean bra. If the police badger your brother to much about what he did be sure he knows that I have pictures to make them back off. He'll understand."

THE DRUNK DETECTIVE

"Oh, I'm sure. You're a detective, I bet you have compromising pics."

"I certainly do. I'll be in touch if I learn anything."

CHAPTER 26

Shortly after two a.m. Dotty staggered into her apartment having drunk away the realization that she never made an anonymous call to have Chen cleaned up. She was sickened, but protecting her own backside trumped the idea of saving his. She sat on her bed and the telephone rang. "Whoever you are, you better be dying?"

"I'm dying to know why you haven't checked in. I was beginning to think you scored cash from the bishop and skipped town."

"Swayze?"

"Who else? So did you get paid?"

"What?"

"The bishop. Jiminy Cricket. Did you make a deal to sell the pictures?"

"Working on that. Treat this like a post-job interview: I'll call you, don't call me." She hung up.

THE DRUNK DETECTIVE

She was stretched on her bed in all of her clothes when her phone rang again.

"Patrick Swayze, Jesus."

"You dreaming of the Dirty Dancing sexy version, or the To Wong Foo Thanks For Everything gay one?" It was Rodriguez.

"I'm mad that you know the entire title." Dotty drew a deep breath. "It's two-thirty a.m."

"Thank you. This the twentieth time I've tried to call both of your numbers and I E-mailed you. I contacted all of the bars you told me about yesterday."

"We gotta talk now?"

"You were truthful, I wouldn't go back to Moriarty's if I were a sane person."

"What's the deal?"

"Homicide, buddy-o-pal. You've left out some details in our prior chats."

Chen. Dotty shot up, moaning with her bones cracking, and groped around for her flask. It wasn't in bed with her. "Shit. Where are you? Downstairs?"

"Hell no. Why would I be there? I'm in Society Hill."

"Society Hill?"

"Society Hill. Is there an echo on the line?"

"What's in Society Hill?"

"Point blank. One dead bishop."

"Bullshit. Sinclair?" She immediately slapped her leg. "Oh, God."

Pause. "You said that faster than a contestant on Family Feud looking to play."

She feverishly looked for her flask. She found it. Drank the one available drop.

"Dotty Davis, you still with me?"

"Yes. I don't know nothing 'bout a dead bishop."

"Funny. You knew his name."

"Lucky guess of a trained dick."

"Well tell me what's next in this case?"

Dotty said nothing.

"Yup, I hear heavy breathing. I need you to meet me..."

"Look, I'm not going to meet you anywhere."

"Meet me at the precinct or I'll have so many police cars on your block to search every apartment including Chen's to fuck with your neighbors. He'll surely kick you out just like your boss did."

"I quit."

"I talked to him, too. He fired you. I can assure you that your day will start quite badly if I have to come there. Two dead clergy from the same parish is looking like one killer. You want to tell me something?"

"Yes. I am not the killer."

"That was something. You own a gun?"

"If you want to call it that. I haven't seen it in weeks." Dotty began to sweat from every pore. Lynch hadn't left her apartment empty-handed after all.

"Rigors in full swing, 'bout six hours. Could be longer. He has powder burns on his face. Killer pressed the gun right to his forehead. We think he knew and expected the murderer."

THE DRUNK DETECTIVE

"I can't hit the LOVE sign in Love Park at point blank range."

"Good, but I'll need you down at the precinct ASAP to run some test on you."

"I'm not in need of any tests. My health is good."

"Your liver is on it's last breath I am sure. Powder burn tests. Prints. Polygraph."

Dotty said, "Oh, that'll clear my name. I'll be there after I report a burglary."

CHAPTER 27

They locked her in a tank with a stiletto murderer, a pair of butch-lesbians accused of extorting and sodimizing a gay club owner, and a farm girl awaiting extradition to Florida to answer charges of conspiracy to commit robbery, home invasion, and breeding horses in a residential zone.

The butch-lesbians minded their own business, and the stiletto killer seemed content laying on the concrete floor rubbing her feet. Her shoes (size 12 Manolo Blahnik pumps) were collected as evidence in a murder. The farm girl befriended Dotty. She ran north of three hundred pounds and close to six-feet-four inches with hair down to her ass, Dotty was not inclined to ignore her. Her name was Alexiah.

"Dotty," she said laying an arm on Dotty's shoulder's forcing her to sag, "you like horses?"

"Not particularly. You can't eat them."

"Click. Clack," said the stiletto murderer.

THE DRUNK DETECTIVE

"You see that bitch face when I punched his ass?" asked one of the butch-lesbians.

"You'd be surprised all of the uses of horses," said Alexiah, pulling Dotty closer to her. "Do you like horses now?"

"Well give me an example?" Dotty's reply was choked.

"Click. Click. Clack," said the stiletto murderer.

"That wasn't nothing compared to when you stuck the pipe up his ass," said the other butch-lesbian.

"Anyway, horses isn't all we got in Florida. We got oranges," Alexiah said. "They give oranges with everything. Ever have orange juice and a plate of orange slices with breakfast?"

"No. That's odd."

"Click. Clack. Click. Clack," said the stiletto murderer.

"We shouldn't have left it up his ass. Your prints may be on it," said the first butch-lesbian. "You twirled that pipe around and round, gaping his hole. He probably loved it."

"What you locked up for, Dotty?" asked Alexiah.

"They say I killed two bishops."

"You're going to hell. Two? Yeah, you're done. God hates you. The whole Catholic diocese will be outside the courthouse when you go for bail."

"Tell me something that I don't know."

"You should get a horse. They never die on you. When they do you can eat them despite what people say."

"Click. Click. Click. Click. Clack!" said the stiletto murderer.

Alexiah was telling Dotty about a sexual escapade with a horse when the turn-key officer came. "Davis."

"Present." Dotty raised her hand.

The cop shook his set of keys and inserted one in the lock. "Let's go. You're out. Your lawyer's here."

"What's his name? I called three in honor of the trinity."

"The deaf one in an orange suit. Looks like a clown. He's been here over the years."

"Oh, Doc Brennan."

"Hey," said one of the butch-lesbians, as the cop was re-locking the bars behind Dotty. "When do we eat?"

"Soon."

"Better be. We need something down the pipeline sooner than later." The other butch-lesbian chuckled.

"Take care of yourself, Dotty," said Alexiah, through the bars. "Don't forget me."

"I seriously doubt it, honey."

Larry Brennan was waiting in the discharge room, along with Sergeant Rodriguez, Lieutenant Boxer, and, behind the desk, another Philadelphia PD officer who had processed Dotty three hours earlier. The officer emptied a manila envelop full of Dotty's valuables onto a wood counter engraved with many other releasees street monikers and checked them off against a list on a clipboard.

"One silver flask."

"Hello, Dotty." Brennan took Dotty's hand in his wet palm. He was a short, Irish man in his seventies, with manicured nails and a hearing aid. He was often mistaken for a fancy dressed private doctor thanks to all of his loud suits.

"What's up, doc? How's Barb?"

"One plastic toothpick holder."

THE DRUNK DETECTIVE

"It's been a while, Dotty. Barb's two wives back. It's Amazing Amy now."

"Oh. Wasn't you married to Francine, too?"

"No, you're thinking Francesca. This one's a cheerleader."

"Wow. Temple U."

"Northeast High. She's barely legal."

"I thought you seemed weak."

"Viagra script only helps so much."

"One pork-bound notebook."

"It's called pig skin. What happened to the other two lawyers that I called."

"Jared Johnson's wanted for child support payments and ducking any new cases just in case the ex-wife proves paternity. Robert Roberts is in intensive care at Einstein Med Center. He forgot to show up for rapper Meek Mills' probation violation hearing last week. Someone reminded him to never miss another court appearance."

"One gold pinky ring."

"Well I'm elated to see you, Doc. Thanks for getting me released."

"One silver pinky ring."

"The sarge and the LT here were scared of my presence so they dropped the absurd accusations."

"One pinky ring, perhaps white gold."

Dotty looked at Rodriguez and Boxer, smiled. Rodriguez grinned and dropped a cigarette butt on the tiled floor. "It's LT Boxer's case."

"One female condom."

"The ME put Sinclair's death at approximately eleven a.m. and two," Boxer said, adjusting a boring clip-on tie. "You were with Luscious Goldberg at eleven-thirty, being fired."

"I quit," she said. "For the record."

"An altar boy at Our Lady of the Rosary says you were at the cathedral before noon and stayed about an hour and a half. Soon after you met my sergeant at the hospital. It's hardly possible a woman of your caliber pulled off a murder with these strict times recorded by trust worthy people."

"I resent that. I'm quite capable, but..."

"I doubt it. You couldn't have been fi..."

"Quit my job."

"With Goldberg and made a perfect route to kill the bishop. That would've required no traffic and all green lights in Center City. I can't hold you."

"One multi-color ascot, Versace," said the police officer behind the desk.

"Well, I gotta go folks."

"Two matchbooks from Dave and Busters and Delilah's Strip Club."

"Before you go, can you be a Barbie doll and tell me about your business with Bishop Sinclair."

"Thirteen .380 slugs, two Canadian pennies, and a Susan B. Anthony dollar piece. Sign on this line."

Dotty signed the receipt and stuffed her belongings into her pockets. "I wanted to give my condolences to the good nun punching her ticket to the Upper Room."

Brennan took off his fedora, ran a finger over his bald head.

"Come on, Dotty, the bishop was killed with your gun."

"And it was stolen from my place."

"Speak up, Dotty."

Dotty gave a wicked glare at her attorney. "I thought this is when you tell me to shut the hell up."

"My batteries died." Brennan removed the hearing aid and smacked it into his palm.

Rodriguez stomped his foot at a new burn mark on his necktie. "I guess this is the end of the road for us, Dotty. Too bad Frankie survived. The case has been assigned to Lieutenant Boxer."

"Tell me he's alive."

Lt. Boxer said, "We do attempt homicides, too. And I know about a fact that you know: there's a connection between who tried to blow up Frankie and who did shoot Bishop Sinclair. You may not tell me today, but I'm coming for you because I know you know that connection."

"I have Sprint, very bad service. I know nothing about good connections. I see you're clairvoyant, though."

"That's fine. You'll get an upgrade."

"Fuck you, Lieutenant."

"Speak up, Dotty," Brennan said.

Dotty snatched the hearing aid out of the lawyer's hand, put it to her lips, and shouted, "Fuck you."

"Oh. Don't worry yourself about that. The bill is coming your way at five-hundred an hour."

CHAPTER 28

Outside of the Round House's cell block, Dotty rushed towards the exit's swinging door and it slammed into her face by a cop entering the building. It was the cop who had spoken with Dotty two mornings ago while she sat in Lynch's hearse next to Sister Tudor.

"Are you OK, ma'am?" The officer asked and warmly placed a hand on Dotty's shoulder.

She covered the bottom of her face, blood leaked from her nose onto her fingers, which were badly in need of a manicure. In a high-pitched voice, she said, "Oh yes, Sir, I am being great, very very great, thank you."

"You don't look all that great."

"I'm great. I always look this way, Sir." Bowing with exaggeration she pulled open the door to flea the police HQ.

"Wait, ma'am. We've met, right?"

"Absolutely not. I would be very very sure had we met. I'm sure."

Outside she leaned against a Channel Six Action News van and blew her nose into some tissue from a reporter. She was occupied cleaning up when a red Dodge Charger pulled into the space behind the van. It's driver put down the passenger window and leaned to look out of it. "Hey, Dotty, you OK?"

"Oh yes, I am just great, very very..." She noticed that it was Naim Butler and her tune changed. "Oh, it's you. I'm good."

"When your cell kept going to VM, I called Goldberg and he told me to call Rodriguez who told me you'd been arrested. Why?"

"Right now, I shouldn't discuss the case. You know, pending investigation red-tape. I'm out for now, can I get a ride?"

"That's why I showed up. Where you going?"

"Find a parking lot. In fact, go to the big one on Market Street between Eighth and Ninth across from the Gallery Mall."

"Do I look like an UBER driver?"

"For now, yes."

They rode for a few blocks in silence. The Charger's engine purred and the tires hissed on the dewy streets. Dotty went through her pockets until she found the pigskin-and-gold notebook she'd removed from the front of Our Lady of the Rosary Church's rectory. She had assumed that perhaps the bishop had dropped it on his way in, but now she guessed the killer dropped it on their way out.

The first five pages were filed with names and numbers recorded in the same print that had sent her an invite to the first meeting. Presumptuously, the bishop's neat script. Dotty recognized some of the local church celebrities, the ones that were questioned on TV about a sex scandal. There were some city officials, and local area celebs, but most were unknown to her. There was a lone number on a page with a 202-area code: Washington, DC.

Naim pulled into the parking lot as Dotty dialed the DC number. Oddly, she felt like some kind of capped-sleuth who had to get to the bottom of a bishop's murder and the almost-murder of a prostitute. This for one simple reason, the bishop was going to pay Dotty's bills for the next thirty years or longer.

"United States Justice Department."

It was a pleasant kind of voice. Dotty said, "Thee US Justice Department in Washington?"

"The one and only, ma'am. Can I help you?"

"Well are we talking the state or the place with the big white buildings?"

"The state of Washington, ma'am, doesn't have a just department. They have rain."

"OK, let me get the man at the top. The Big Cheese."

"You mean the woman, Attorney General, Loretta Scalia."

Dammit, man. "Well, if she's available, yes."

"Your name?"

"Just tell her the City of Brotherly Love is calling."

"Okey-dokey. One moment, City of Brotherly Love."

Dotty was placed on hold. After some elevator music bored her, a raspy, university-loaded voice she knew vaguely from television broadcasts came on the line.

"Lynch, I told you to never call me here." She hung up.

Dotty tossed her phone on the dashboard, and said, "Wow."

"What happened? Who was that?"

"The Justice Department. Seems they're in on this Church killing spree. I'm wondering the connection to Frankie Robinson now."

"Where to next?"

"You can't hang wit me, kid. I'm dangerous right now."

"You were yesterday, too. And the days and months before that." He started the car, and then turned to Dotty. "Let me thank you for the advice. Scott Dempsey was in a hotel room with a dirty blonde. He came clean about the thefts. Mr. Goldberg gave me a bonus."

"I bet he loved that."

"He acted like I was problematic. But he made up the bonus rule, so he had to pay up. He had the audacity to put a reprimand in my file for violating his other company rule."

"Screw his rules. If his reprimands were bullets, I'd be Swiss cheese."

"That wasn't a compliment. I invested the money with a Wall Street broker already. I've got big ambitions, Dotty."

Dotty's spider-senses perked up. "I see you know how to prioritize. Glad I could be of service to your goals." Naim began to back out of the space. Dotty cracked a window. "What are you going to do now?"

"I am still wondering."

"Do not do that. It's dangerous and hurts the brain."

"Let me tag along with you on this case. You can teach me some pointers. You know about being a great investigator."

"There's no case. I don't even have a job."

"You can work for yourself. You don't need an agency."

"I just got out of jail."

"Many great woman went to jail. Men sleuths, too. Sherlock Holmes..."

"A wuss. He didn't do anything and they'd have his ass at the Round House, too. Anyway, he's fictional."

"No shit, Sherlock. I was just hoping."

"I don't know, kid." Dotty said and popped in a toothpick. "Maybe there is something you can help me with. I've read something in your personnel file."

"Perfect. What's that?"

"Hold up, don't get your panties pooped in. No pay, just experience."

"What you need me to do?"

Dotty smiled. "You know why you were arrested in Chicago. I need that expertise."

THE DRUNK DETECTIVE

CHAPTER 29

"Get away from me, Dotty," Swayze said, sitting in a semi-circular booth in the Circ Restaurant inside of the downtown Marriott Hotel. He wore a white bib with a Maine lobster on it, and the remains of the same life form lay on his plate, classical music played very low in the background.

"Your secretary told me that I could find you here. I need your help."

"Tell my secretary she's fired. Who's this with you?"

"Naim Butler. He's an intern with the agency from U of Penn Law School."

"Hello, sir," Naim said. "I've heard so much about you."

"You bitch," Swayze said to Dotty. "It had better been all nice. I see no one has killed you, yet." Swayze picked out some of the lobster's brain with a miniature fork.

"That's why we're here."

"Oh, I'll kill you after I'm done with the lobster."

"Such a comedian, Swayze." Dotty and Naim slid into the booth and a waiter handed them menus. "Isn't you got any cheap burgers?"

"The ground sirloin here is good," Naim said. "And it's *don't*, ma'am."

"You can afford it. A firm sent you here from New York and pay for your Ivy League schooling. I'm sure they're paying for you to have fine dining. I don't have that luxury." She returned her menu to the waiter, and said, "I'll have what he just praised. Well done with a slice of Velveeta. None of that provolone crap."

"And to drink?"

"What's on tap?"

"There's a full assortment of imported beers."

"Nothing from Mexico. It makes me piss all damn day, and mine is just starting this late. Bring me a Corona in a can. I found a nose hair in a bottle once," she confided to Swayze and Naim. "What do you think, he does it to the busboy, or the busboy does it to him?"

"Jesus Christ, Dotty." That was Naim. "You can't be homophobic."

"You see the way those hips sway when they carry trays. Waiting tables was made for a woman." She took a gulp of Swayze's water. "So here's what I need from you two."

"Oh boy," Swayze said.

"Look, you're still a whiz with computers?"

"Never was."

"That's why Naim is here. He was in jail for hacking credit card numbers from Chance Bank. Did hard fed time, now he's on track."

THE DRUNK DETECTIVE

"There is a God," Swayze said.

Dotty said, "We need to use a computer at your job."

"Why the hell is that?"

"Simply put. To bust into the files at the Justice Department. The Chinese do it, so can Mr. Butler, here."

"You're talking about the Justice Department in Washington, D.C.?"

"They don't have one in Washington state. I asked. They have rain."

"You idiot."

"Oh well, I've been called worse. I need to know why the AG would want to kill a male prostitute and a bishop, and what it all has to do with a dead nun."

"Loretta Scalia, as in the first African-American female AG with an Italian last name?"

"That's funny, right?"

"Their files. I can break into them," Naim said.

Dotty's ground sirloin came, on a big plate with a kid's portion of broccoli and wild rice?" Dotty asked. "People pay twenty-eight-dollars for this. Am I supposed to eat it or take a picture of it and post it on Instagram?"

"You have an Instagram?" Naim asked in spite of himself.

"You can shove it up your rude ass for all I care." The waiter left.

"He gets no tip," Dotty told Swayze. "He forgot my beverage."

"You said that like you ordered a Sprite."

"Why do you like the attorney general for murder?" Swayze asked.

"When I called there, because I found the number in a notebook that I stole from Bishop Sinclair..."

"You're going straight to hell."

"...I said it was the City of Brotherly Love calling, Scalia came on the line and called me Lynch." Dotty spoke whole chewing ground sirloin. "Lynch is the one that booby-trapped the gigolo's apartment. That will be on tonight's news thanks to Naim who's banging a production assistant there."

"Dotty!"

Swayze said, "That was on the radio this morning. Cops claim to have a suspect awaiting arraignment."

"That was me, you dope. I was sprung not to long ago. So can we use the computer?"

"The AG has all kinds of server security codes, I doubt lover boy here can get in as easily as he gets into pants."

"See that, Dotty. You're giving people the wrong impression of me."

"He can. Did you know last month a teenager obviously bored in Lincoln, Nebraska tapped into the Pentagon and sent a thousand cases of Magnum condoms and KY-Jelly to Syria."

"Quite the international care giving effort it it cuts down on the number of little Islamic State babies being born," Swayze said.

"This is about money, Swayze," Naim said.

"Yup," said Dotty. "If the bishop was willing to pay on his low wages, what do you think a member of the president's cabinet would pay up. All them assholes down there want to be president."

THE DRUNK DETECTIVE

"Have you asked yourself why Scalia would care how a Philly priest kicked the bucket?"

"That's why I need to help Dotty hack into the AG's E-mails. It's hard to blackmail someone without the goods," Naim said.

"This could be a million pay out," Dotty said.

"Dollars," Naim added. "Hell, BMWs."

"From this moment on it's all fifty-fifty," Dotty said.

Swayze raised his eyebrows. "You cross me, Dotty-O-Pal, and I'll have your ass for breakfast."

"I would never stiff a friend. I resent the accusation." Dotty finished her meal and stood. Naim followed suit. "Don't forget what I said about the tip."

* * *

Naim dropped Dotty off at her apartment. She planned to have him pick her up later near closing time for Swayze's bank, so that they could slip into the back door and do what they had to do. Sitting on the front steps of her apartment building was Hank Robinson in a puffy Eagles NFL jacket, complimentary fitted ball cap pulled down to his eyebrows, and gaudy sunglasses.

Dotty said, "I didn't recognize you. Thought you were a thug rapper."

He laughed. "I didn't know that you lived next door to a sleazy massage parlor."

"Now you do. What are you doing here?"

"Waiting on you. I really need to talk to you," he said, and looked deeply into her eyes.

"Well, I am all ears. Let me go straighten up my apartment. It's a mess. I'll all you in a sec to come on up."

Racing to her apartment, Dotty got right to straightening up her apartment. She put chairs and tables upright, flipped over damaged cushions to disguise the holes. She even mopped with some disinfectant, something that she never did. Finally, she emptied the dregs of four different kinds of liquor from nine bottles into a tall glass and gulped that down her throat. The empties went into a garbage bag with the rest of the trash, and then out of a window aimed at a dumpster in the alley. It landed with a thud, sending a cat scurrying and just missing a bum. She then went downstairs, to collect her guest. The dregs had provoked her appetite; the steak did nothing.

* * *

Upstairs, Hank gasped at the door to Dotty's lair.

"Bad termite problem," she said, unlocking it.

He went in first and walked through a path that Dotty had cleared to her bedroom. He reached for the light switch, Dotty screamed, "No!" and grabbed his bicep. She sniffed for gas before flipping the switch. "Can't be to careful," she said.

"My place never looked this bag on campus as a freshman. You need a man.

"What're you, broccoli?" she asked at the bedroom door.

"I mean to clean for you. This place looks like it's been ransacked."

"It could use a light dusting." She picked up a destroyed pillow, releasing a cloud of feathers into the air. "You thirsty/"

"A little. What you have?"

THE DRUNK DETECTIVE

She lifted a bed sheet and a bottle with liquid in it popped into the air. She caught it, opened it, and smelled. "Looks like vodka."

"I'll take it. What I want to do, I shouldn't be sober for." His tone slipped to seductive and she turned to face him. "Let's drink this." He took the bottle from her.

* * *

It was light outside when Dotty rolled out of the bed onto her hands and knees, grabbed the dresser to stand, and stumbled naked to the bathroom. She flicked on the light and looked absurdly at herself in the mirror above the sink. Her breasts hung down near her stomach and were depressingly flat. Her skin tone was pale and pink-colored. She threw water on her face, before a quick wash over her pertinent parts, and then crept back into the bedroom.

She kicked the door and stubbed a toe and bit down on her lip to avoid screaming. She was deathly afraid of waking Hank, who was breathing heavily on his back with his eyes shut and the sheet pulled down exposing a chiseled chest and stomach. He looked serene and ready for another round. *This must run in the Robinson family*, she thought. Immediately after Dotty gathered herself, she put his fitted cap on her head. She smiled looking in the mirror at herself.

When she was done parading around in the mirror on her dresser, he said, "Having fun?"

"I night buy one of these. We'll be twinning. Or to wear to the Eagles games, of course."

He chuckled.

"What's funny?" she asked, sitting the hat down on the dresser.

"You are. When you're naked."

She sat on the side of the bed, and smiled at him. "Well, I don't hit the Zumba classes or run. I own a car."

"I meant the hat."

She grinned. "Oh, good thing I took it off."

He sat up and pulled on his boxers. He checked his watch, and then shot off the bed. "Shit."

"What's wrong?"

"I had a class this afternoon. I have to go."

"It's not polite to eat and run," she said. "Come back to bed."

"I really can't. I have to get to a class late."

"I understand," she said, and then slipped in her clothing, too. "I guess I better let you go."

"We'll meet up again. Call me."

"You never got around to telling me why you came here in the first place."

"Well, you've taken my mind off my problems, and I don't even know why I came. Glad that I did stop by, though." He winked at her. "Bye, Ms. Dotty."

Hank left and she decided to straighten up her apartment. *He may come back. I did put it on him.* After minimal work, she became hungry, and said, "Fuck this shit. He can do this. That is what he said. I gotta eat to pack back on those calories that I lost."

She dressed—ugly X-mas sweater and pajama bottoms, loafers without socks—and walked out of the door.

"Good afternoon, Mrs. Lombardo," she said as she spun around the second floor landing.

THE DRUNK DETECTIVE

The blind bat was perched at the bottom of the stairs looked up, fixed her glasses on her nose, and pointed a pale finger. "That's her!"

Then Dotty saw the officer who had seen her in the car with Sister Tudor and the same one that busted her nose. In front of them the door of Chen's apartment where Dotty had stashed his body was ajar. The officer un-holstered his revolver.

"Freeze!"

He had sounded like a TV cop, and Dotty guessed that's where he's gotten the line. No criminal had ever froze on that command. Obviously, innocent people didn't freeze either, Dotty turned around and was running up the stairs she'd just came down. The police officer gave chase.

On her floor, Dotty didn't bother to try to locate her keys, she said eff this and went through what was left of the door. The window used for a trash shoot by her a moment ago was still open.

Without second guessing, she climbed over the sill, was perched there for a second, then as soon as she heard the footsteps enter her place she pushed off. She was a woman without wings, but flew for two seconds. Then she slammed into the ground with her knees in her chest, on top of a dead rat, the cat she scared away earlier may have caught and all but one of the bottles she had thrown out moments before.

When she was able to refocus, she saw a homeless woman right outside the dumpster. The woman had the other bottle tipped upside down and was rubbing at the insides of the neck with a crusty tongue. Dotty recognized her as a panhandler outside of the McDonald's on Market Street.

MARY JEAN CURRY

The woman popped her lips and balled up her face. "You actually drank this piss?" she asked.

CHAPTER 30

The only jarring difference between the woman and Dotty worth noting was the woman's jacket was a green and yellow Green Bay Packers number covered in a patina of filth. Dotty's blazer was a more conservative black polyester.

"You got a hover board or something 'cause you get around the Center City area, I see," Dotty said. "I thought bums stayed closer to where they ate and panhandled."

"Who the hell you calling a bum? Do I look like a bum? I am not any body's bum."

"What are you, Ms. Universe?"

"When the Christmas lights get put away, I am homeless."

"OK, Homeless, can you drive a car?"

"Is Putin a communist?"

"I take that as a yes."

"I wasn't always like this."

"Homeless, I have twenty easy bucks for you. Wanna make a quick buck?"

"Did Martin Luther King win a Nobel Peace Prize?"

"You must get rest in the main library on Vine."

"Yup, you can find me between African-American studies and Russian History on Monday's," she said, smiling with five teeth that had never been close to each other.

Dotty held up a twenty-dollar-bill. "Let's exchange jackets."

Homeless looked skeptically, put down the empty bottle and felt one of Dotty's lapels between thumb and forefinger. "I'm used to foreign wool and Asian denim," she said. "But OK."

They switched outerwear and Dotty handed her the bill and the car keys. "There's a fancy Mercedes parked in front of this apartment building. Get to it and burn rubber. Someone will chase you."

"Cops or robbers?"

"Cops."

"OK, I don't mess with the South Philly Italian mob. Where should I leave it?"

"How 'bout Canada? I don't care, it ain't mine and the owner has much bigger problems." Dotty heard keys and the squawk of a walkie-talkie entering the alley. "Get out of here."

Homeless shrugged, flicked a banana peel off the sleeve of Dotty's blazer, and jumped over the dumpster. Dotty heard the officer shout, "Freeze!" again and then there were galloping footsteps. A shot rang out and made the dumpster ring as loud as the Liberty Bell. She then heard more police footsteps.

THE DRUNK DETECTIVE

She backed against a wall and then jumped inside the dumpster as the cops ran by. She heard the Mercedes revved up and burned rubber.

Ten minutes passed before, she grabbed the top of the dumpster and peeked over the side. The cat that she had scared off earlier hissed at her between licking the interior of a discarded tuna can. Otherwise she was alone. She climbed out. The loud jacket had began to make her itch. At the length of the alley she came out on Spring Garden Street, where a few cabs passed her up until a Saudi with an expired VISA driving a newer Yellow Cab stopped for her.

"I gotta get twenty up front, ma'am, to take you any where."

Dotty dug into her pocket and showed him some cash. She handed the driver a ten.

"Where to, ma'am? 'Cause this won't get you far."

Dotty hesitated. She had time to kill before she was supposed to meet Swayze in a city with cops that were tracking her for murder. "U of Penn," she said. "I'll tell you where to drop me exactly when we get over there."

"That's normally how it works."

For Dotty the ride across downtown was magical. She was whisked by corporate buildings that ran along JFK Boulevard until they reached 30th Street Station, all the while the cab driver (a devout Muslim) avoided blasphemies while cursing every driver that cross lanes or turned without using a signal. As she text Naim Butler, they shot over to Market Street and passed Drexel University before they reached the University of Penn Law Library with a cop car just a car behind them. She had him pull over with the meter reading: $9.75.

"Keep the change," she said leaving the driver a quarter tip for his harboring a fugitive.

She walked a block up Walnut Street to Naim's dorm and he was waiting in the lobby for her. When he noticed the Green Bay Packers jacket he cringed.

"Where to, ma'am? 'Cause this won't get you far."

Should've gotten an Uber. Dotty hesitated. She had time to kill before she was supposed to meet Swayze in a city with cops that were tracking her for murder. "U of Penn," she said. "I'll tell you where to drop me exactly when we get over there." *Just in case you're an operative.*

"That's normally how it works."

"Just drive, asshole."

For Dotty the ride across downtown was magical. She was whisked by corporate buildings that ran along JFK Boulevard until they reached 30th Street Station, all the while the cab driver—a devout Muslim—avoid blasphemies while cursing every driver that crossed lanes or turned without using a signal. As she text Naim Butler, they shot over to Market Street and passed Drexel University, before they reached the University of Penn Law Library. With Dotty's luck, a cop car pulled behind them. She had him pull over with the meter reading $9.75.

"Keep the change," she said, leaving the driver a quarter tip for his harboring an innocent fugitive.

She walked a block up Walnut Street to Naim's dorm and he was and he was waiting in the lobby for her. When he noticed the Green Bay Packers jacket, he cringed. "You need to get rid of the jacket. In Eagles Nation you stick out a lot and with the whole PPD gunning for you, I doubt you want that kind of attention."

THE DRUNK DETECTIVE

"Keep it down. Jesus," she said, tossing the jacket on a seat in the lobby as they walked to a corner with a bank of pay phones. "Do these work?"

"Yes." He was laughing.

"Anything to drink?"

"Vending machines. All Pepsi products."

"Pepsi? I was thinking more like bourbon or vodka."

"I'm not a drinker. I could go get you hard liquor, though."

"Hard liquor. You're such a nerd. Don't bother," she said, eyeing every student suspiciously as they ebbed through the lobby to their dorm rooms.

"OK, so what's the plan? My head is full of Child Psychology after class."

"Mine, too. What time is it? My watch was ruined breaking my fall from grace."

"Nearly five."

They turned to the thirty-six inch screen TV on the wall. The news fanned a BREAKING NEWS banner across the screen, interrupting Barb "Hurricane" Smith's weather predictions. "This just in..." said the anchor.

"Dotty?"

"Quiet."

"The owner of an adult massage parlor..."

"Is there any other kind?"

"...was discovered dead in his apartment an hour ago, the victim of what appears to be strangulation. Lee Chen, age seventy-four..."

"What now, Dotty?"

"Hush, Naim."

"…a tenant, who called police. Police sought a suspect from the apartment building, who fled and escaped in a new model blue Mercedes…"

"Dotty! I thought you were in a taxi?"

"…suspect's name hasn't been released. We will have more, but now for our update with the sex party at the home of the Temple U lacrosse team." The anchor's face dissolved to a close-up of a beat reporter outside of the team's home holding a box of Lifestyle condoms.

'You didn't do him, did you?" Naim asked.

"No, I ain't been to Temple U in years."

"You know I am talking about Chen. You need to grow up."

"Some murdered named, Lynch, I been telling you about did the old man. The old bag from my building saw me moving the body."

"Oh, wow. Today?"

"A day ago, My bad, this just never came up in conversation."

"You're funny. What about the gigolo? He talking?"

Dotty scratched her left elbow. "You got Lysol around here. I need to get rid of these germs."

"No. Answer my question, Dotty."

She shrugged. "I'm not sure."

"This is crazy. How'd the hell you go from being a drunk detective—well, PI—to being involved in all of this?"

"I detect some shade in that comment, hun bun. Simple. A damn nun sewed her royal oats in a Mandingo warriors bed

THE DRUNK DETECTIVE

in my building. I got rid of her. Quietly, by the way. Now this Lynch clown wants to get rid of me, but Chen got in the damn way."

"Why not just tell the police all of this?"

"Too problematic. Chen was strangled in my apartment. I found him, and kindly took him to his place."

"Doesn't look good. But, hey, I'm just in law school."

"Who you telling?"

"You moved two dead bodies and told the police about neither. I mean, I am no lawyer, but my TV lawyer instincts are telling me you're in deep shit."

"Would you have told on yourself?"

"I'm a black ex-con with a rap sheet worthy of praise. Imagine it."

"Look, Butler, the bishop is dead, too. I'm pretty sure, Loretta Scalia sicced Lynch on Chen, Frankie and the bishop, but I don't know why. We will find out when you get into Scalia's computer."

"Let's do this," he said, looking at his watch. "It's that time. Wait here while I grab my car from the garage. Don't need anyone seeing you roaming the campus. They have that facial recognition crap included with the surveillance.

Just as Naim walked away, Dotty was approached by Hank Robinson.

"What are you doing here, Hankie Pankie?" she asked, fixing her hair.

"I should ask you that. I go to school here, remember?"

"Right. I found out some things about who may be responsible for hurting your brother. Turns out," she said, covering

her mouth, "well, I can't tell you right now, but I will say that there's a chance that DC is involved."

"Who's he?"

"The Government."

"Oh, Big Brother. That's fair, my brother hasn't filled out a W-2 in ages."

She giggled. "Ok, but this isn't about him not paying taxes in years. It could be apart of the problem, though." She heard a car horn and looked out and saw Naim waving at her. "I have to go."

"OK, but please find out who hurt my brother."

"I'll keep you posted."

"You have the Post-It already?" He smiled.

She blushed. "As a matter of fact, I do," she said, winked and then backed up. "I gotta run." She turned around and ran out of the building. Out of the corner of her eye she saw the Green Bay Packers jacket walking up the street. Someone pushing a shopping cart was wearing it.

THE DRUNK DETECTIVE

CHAPTER 31

"Get away from me, Dotty," Swayze said, sitting in a semi-circular booth in the Circ Restaurant inside of the downtown Marriott Hotel. He wore a white bib with a Maine lobster on it, and the remains of the same life form lay on his plate, classical music played very low in the background.

"Your secretary told me that I could find you here. I need your help."

"Tell my secretary she's fired. Who's this with you?"

"Naim Butler. He's an intern with the agency from U of Penn Law School."

"Hello, sir," Naim said. "I've heard so much about you."

"You bitch," Swayze said to Dotty. "It had better been all nice. I see no one has killed you, yet." Swayze picked out some of the lobster's brain with a miniature fork.

"That's why we're here."

"Oh, I'll kill you after I'm done with the lobster."

"Such a comedian, Swayze." Dotty and Naim slid into the booth and a waiter handed them menus. "Isn't you got any cheap burgers?"

"The ground sirloin here is good," Naim said. "And it's *don't*, ma'am."

"You can afford it. A firm sent you here from New York and pay for your Ivy League schooling. I'm sure they're paying for you to have fine dining. I don't have that luxury." She returned her menu to the waiter, and said, "I'll have what he just praised. Well done with a slice of Velveeta. None of that provolone crap."

"And to drink?"

"What's on tap?"

"There's a full assortment of imported beers."

"Nothing from Mexico. It makes me piss all damn day, and mine is just starting this late. Bring me a Corona in a can. I found a nose hair in a bottle once," she confided to Swayze and Naim. "What do you think, he does it to the busboy, or the busboy does it to him?"

"Jesus Christ, Dotty." That was Naim. "You can't be homophobic."

"You see the way those hips sway when they carry trays. Waiting tables was made for a woman." She took a gulp of Swayze's water. "So here's what I need from you two."

"Oh boy," Swayze said.

"Look, you're still a whiz with computers?"

"Never was."

"That's why Naim is here. He was in jail for hacking credit card numbers from Chance Bank. Did hard fed time, now he's on track."

"There is a God," Swayze said.

Dotty said, "We need to use a computer at your job."

"Why the hell is that?"

"Simply put. To bust into the files at the Justice Department. The Chinese do it, so can Mr. Butler, here."

"You're talking about the Justice Department in Washington, D.C.?"

"They don't have one in Washington state. I asked. They have rain."

"You idiot."

"Oh well, I've been called worse. I need to know why the AG would want to kill a male prostitute and a bishop, and what it all has to do with a dead nun."

"Loretta Scalia, as in the first African-American female AG with an Italian last name?"

"That's funny, right?"

"Their files. I can break into them," Naim said.

Dotty's ground sirloin came, on a big plate with a kid's portion of broccoli and wild rice?" Dotty asked. "People pay twenty-eight-dollars for this. Am I supposed to eat it or take a picture of it and post it on Instagram?"

"You have an Instagram?" Naim asked in spite of himself.

"You can shove it up your rude ass for all I care." The waiter left.

"He gets no tip," Dotty told Swayze. "He forgot my beverage."

"You said that like you ordered a Sprite."

"Why do you like the attorney general for murder?" Swayze asked.

"When I called there, because I found the number in a notebook that I stole from Bishop Sinclair..."

"You're going straight to hell."

"...I said it was the City of Brotherly Love calling, Scalia came on the line and called me Lynch." Dotty spoke whole chewing ground sirloin. "Lynch is the one that booby-trapped the gigolo's apartment. That will be on tonight's news thanks to Naim who's banging a production assistant there."

"Dotty!"

Swayze said, "That was on the radio this morning. Cops claim to have a suspect awaiting arraignment."

"That was me, you dope. I was sprung not to long ago. So can we use the computer?"

"The AG has all kinds of server security codes, I doubt lover boy here can get in as easily as he gets into pants."

"See that, Dotty. You're giving people the wrong impression of me."

"He can. Did you know last month a teenager obviously bored in Lincoln, Nebraska tapped into the Pentagon and sent a thousand cases of Magnum condoms and KY-Jelly to Syria."

"Quite the international care giving effort it it cuts down on the number of little Islamic State babies being born," Swayze said.

"This is about money, Swayze," Naim said.

"Yup," said Dotty. "If the bishop was willing to pay on his low wages, what do you think a member of the president's cabinet would pay up. All them assholes down there want to be president."

THE DRUNK DETECTIVE

"Have you asked yourself why Scalia would care how a Philly priest kicked the bucket?"

"That's why I need to help Dotty hack into the AG's E-mails. It's hard to blackmail someone without the goods," Naim said.

"This could be a million pay out," Dotty said.

"Dollars," Naim added. "Hell, BMWs."

"From this moment on it's all fifty-fifty," Dotty said.

Swayze raised his eyebrows. "You cross me, Dotty-O-Pal, and I'll have your ass for breakfast."

"I would never stiff a friend. I resent the accusation." Dotty finished her meal and stood. Naim followed suit. "Don't forget what I said about the tip."

* * *

Naim dropped Dotty off at her apartment. She planned to have him pick her up later near closing time for Swayze's bank, so that they could slip into the back door and do what they had to do. Sitting on the front steps of her apartment building was Hank Robinson in a puffy Eagles NFL jacket, complimentary fitted ball cap pulled down to his eyebrows, and gaudy sunglasses.

Dotty said, "I didn't recognize you. Thought you were a thug rapper."

He laughed. "I didn't know that you lived next door to a sleazy massage parlor."

"Now you do. What are you doing here?"

"Waiting on you. I really need to talk to you," he said, and looked deeply into her eyes.

"Well, I am all ears. Let me go straighten up my apartment. It's a mess. I'll all you in a sec to come on up."

Racing to her apartment, Dotty got right to straightening up her apartment. She put chairs and tables upright, flipped over damaged cushions to disguise the holes. She even mopped with some disinfectant, something that she never did. Finally, she emptied the dregs of four different kinds of liquor from nine bottles into a tall glass and gulped that down her throat. The empties went into a garbage bag with the rest of the trash, and then out of a window aimed at a dumpster in the alley. It landed with a thud, sending a cat scurrying and just missing a bum. She then went downstairs, to collect her guest. The dregs had provoked her appetite; the steak did nothing.

* * *

Upstairs, Hank gasped at the door to Dotty's lair.

"Bad termite problem," she said, unlocking it.

He went in first and walked through a path that Dotty had cleared to her bedroom. He reached for the light switch, Dotty screamed, "No!" and grabbed his bicep. She sniffed for gas before flipping the switch. "Can't be to careful," she said.

"My place never looked this bag on campus as a freshman. You need a man.

"What're you, broccoli?" she asked at the bedroom door.

"I mean to clean for you. This place looks like it's been ransacked."

"It could use a light dusting." She picked up a destroyed pillow, releasing a cloud of feathers into the air. "You thirsty/"

"A little. What you have?"

THE DRUNK DETECTIVE

She lifted a bed sheet and a bottle with liquid in it popped into the air. She caught it, opened it, and smelled. "Looks like vodka."

"I'll take it. What I want to do, I shouldn't be sober for." His tone slipped to seductive and she turned to face him. "Let's drink this." He took the bottle from her.

* * *

It was light outside when Dotty rolled out of the bed onto her hands and knees, grabbed the dresser to stand, and stumbled naked to the bathroom. She flicked on the light and looked absurdly at herself in the mirror above the sink. Her breasts hung down near her stomach and were depressingly flat. Her skin tone was pale and pink-colored. She threw water on her face, before a quick wash over her pertinent parts, and then crept back into the bedroom.

She kicked the door and stubbed a toe and bit down on her lip to avoid screaming. She was deathly afraid of waking Hank, who was breathing heavily on his back with his eyes shut and the sheet pulled down exposing a chiseled chest and stomach. He looked serene and ready for another round. *This must run in the Robinson family*, she thought. Immediately after Dotty gathered herself, she put his fitted cap on her head. She smiled looking in the mirror at herself.

When she was done parading around in the mirror on her dresser, he said, "Having fun?"

"I night buy one of these. We'll be twinning. Or to wear to the Eagles games, of course."

He chuckled.

"What's funny?" she asked, sitting the hat down on the dresser.

"You are. When you're naked."

She sat on the side of the bed, and smiled at him. "Well, I don't hit the Zumba classes or run. I own a car."

"I meant the hat."

She grinned. "Oh, good thing I took it off."

He sat up and pulled on his boxers. He checked his watch, and then shot off the bed. "Shit."

"What's wrong?"

"I had a class this afternoon. I have to go."

"It's not polite to eat and run," she said. "Come back to bed."

"I really can't. I have to get to a class late."

"I understand," she said, and then slipped in her clothing, too. "I guess I better let you go."

"We'll meet up again. Call me."

"You never got around to telling me why you came here in the first place."

"Well, you've taken my mind off my problems, and I don't even know why I came. Glad that I did stop by, though." He winked at her. "Bye, Ms. Dotty."

Hank left and she decided to straighten up her apartment. *He may come back. I did put it on him.* After minimal work, she became hungry, and said, "Fuck this shit. He can do this. That is what he said. I gotta eat to pack back on those calories that I lost."

She dressed—ugly X-mas sweater and pajama bottoms, loafers without socks—and walked out of the door.

"Good afternoon, Mrs. Lombardo," she said as she spun around the second floor landing.

THE DRUNK DETECTIVE

The blind bat was perched at the bottom of the stairs looked up, fixed her glasses on her nose, and pointed a pale finger. "That's her!"

Then Dotty saw the officer who had seen her in the car with Sister Tudor and the same one that busted her nose. In front of them the door of Chen's apartment where Dotty had stashed his body was ajar. The officer un-holstered his revolver.

"Freeze!"

He had sounded like a TV cop, and Dotty guessed that's where he's gotten the line. No criminal had ever froze on that command. Obviously, innocent people didn't freeze either, Dotty turned around and was running up the stairs she'd just came down. The police officer gave chase.

On her floor, Dotty didn't bother to try to locate her keys, she said eff this and went through what was left of the door. The window used for a trash shoot by her a moment ago was still open.

Without second guessing, she climbed over the sill, was perched there for a second, then as soon as she heard the footsteps enter her place she pushed off. She was a woman without wings, but flew for two seconds. Then she slammed into the ground with her knees in her chest, on top of a dead rat, the cat she scared away earlier may have caught and all but one of the bottles she had thrown out moments before.

When she was able to refocus, she saw a homeless woman right outside the dumpster. The woman had the other bottle tipped upside down and was rubbing at the insides of the neck with a crusty tongue. Dotty recognized her as a panhandler outside of the McDonald's on Market Street.

MARY JEAN CURRY

The woman popped her lips and balled up her face. "You actually drank this piss?" she asked.

THE DRUNK DETECTIVE

CHAPTER 32

The only jarring difference between the woman and Dotty worth noting was the woman's jacket was a green and yellow Green Bay Packers number covered in a patina of filth. Dotty's blazer was a more conservative black polyester.

"You got a hover board or something 'cause you get around the Center City area, I see," Dotty said. "I thought bums stayed closer to where they ate and panhandled."

"Who the hell you calling a bum? Do I look like a bum? I am not any body's bum."

"What are you, Ms. Universe?"

"When the Christmas lights get put away, I am homeless."

"OK, Homeless, can you drive a car?"

"Is Putin a communist?"

"I take that as a yes."

"I wasn't always like this."

"Homeless, I have twenty easy bucks for you. Wanna make a quick buck?"

"Did Martin Luther King win a Nobel Peace Prize?"

"You must get rest in the main library on Vine."

"Yup, you can find me between African-American studies and Russian History on Monday's," she said, smiling with five teeth that had never been close to each other.

Dotty held up a twenty-dollar-bill. "Let's exchange jackets."

Homeless looked skeptically, put down the empty bottle and felt one of Dotty's lapels between thumb and forefinger. "I'm used to foreign wool and Asian denim," she said. "But OK."

They switched outerwear and Dotty handed her the bill and the car keys. "There's a fancy Mercedes parked in front of this apartment building. Get to it and burn rubber. Someone will chase you."

"Cops or robbers?"

"Cops."

"OK, I don't mess with the South Philly Italian mob. Where should I leave it?"

"How 'bout Canada? I don't care, it ain't mine and the owner has much bigger problems." Dotty heard keys and the squawk of a walkie-talkie entering the alley. "Get out of here."

Homeless shrugged, flicked a banana peel off the sleeve of Dotty's blazer, and jumped over the dumpster. Dotty heard the officer shout, "Freeze!" again and then there were galloping footsteps. A shot rang out and made the dumpster ring as loud as the Liberty Bell. She then heard more police footsteps.

THE DRUNK DETECTIVE

She backed against a wall and then jumped inside the dumpster as the cops ran by. She heard the Mercedes revved up and burned rubber.

Ten minutes passed before, she grabbed the top of the dumpster and peeked over the side. The cat that she had scared off earlier hissed at her between licking the interior of a discarded tuna can. Otherwise she was alone. She climbed out. The loud jacket had began to make her itch. At the length of the alley she came out on Spring Garden Street, where a few cabs passed her up until a Saudi with an expired VISA driving a newer Yellow Cab stopped for her.

"I gotta get twenty up front, ma'am, to take you any where."

Dotty dug into her pocket and showed him some cash. She handed the driver a ten.

"Where to, ma'am? 'Cause this won't get you far."

Dotty hesitated. She had time to kill before she was supposed to meet Swayze in a city with cops that were tracking her for murder. "U of Penn," she said. "I'll tell you where to drop me exactly when we get over there."

"That's normally how it works."

For Dotty the ride across downtown was magical. She was whisked by corporate buildings that ran along JFK Boulevard until they reached 30th Street Station, all the while the cab driver (a devout Muslim) avoided blasphemies while cursing every driver that cross lanes or turned without using a signal. As she text Naim Butler, they shot over to Market Street and passed Drexel University before they reached the University of Penn Law Library with a cop car just a car behind them. She had him pull over with the meter reading: $9.75.

"Keep the change," she said leaving the driver a quarter tip for his harboring a fugitive.

She walked a block up Walnut Street to Naim's dorm and he was waiting in the lobby for her. When he noticed the Green Bay Packers jacket he cringed.

"Where to, ma'am? 'Cause this won't get you far."

Should've gotten an Uber. Dotty hesitated. She had time to kill before she was supposed to meet Swayze in a city with cops that were tracking her for murder. "U of Penn," she said. "I'll tell you where to drop me exactly when we get over there." *Just in case you're an operative.*

"That's normally how it works."

"Just drive, asshole."

For Dotty the ride across downtown was magical. She was whisked by corporate buildings that ran along JFK Boulevard until they reached 30th Street Station, all the while the cab driver—a devout Muslim—avoid blasphemies while cursing every driver that crossed lanes or turned without using a signal. As she text Naim Butler, they shot over to Market Street and passed Drexel University, before they reached the University of Penn Law Library. With Dotty's luck, a cop car pulled behind them. She had him pull over with the meter reading $9.75.

"Keep the change," she said, leaving the driver a quarter tip for his harboring an innocent fugitive.

She walked a block up Walnut Street to Naim's dorm and he was and he was waiting in the lobby for her. When he noticed the Green Bay Packers jacket, he cringed. "You need to get rid of the jacket. In Eagles Nation you stick out a lot and with the whole PPD gunning for you, I doubt you want that kind of attention."

THE DRUNK DETECTIVE

"Keep it down. Jesus," she said, tossing the jacket on a seat in the lobby as they walked to a corner with a bank of pay phones. "Do these work?"

"Yes." He was laughing.

"Anything to drink?"

"Vending machines. All Pepsi products."

"Pepsi? I was thinking more like bourbon or vodka."

"I'm not a drinker. I could go get you hard liquor, though."

"Hard liquor. You're such a nerd. Don't bother," she said, eyeing every student suspiciously as they ebbed through the lobby to their dorm rooms.

"OK, so what's the plan? My head is full of Child Psychology after class."

"Mine, too. What time is it? My watch was ruined breaking my fall from grace."

"Nearly five."

They turned to the thirty-six inch screen TV on the wall. The news fanned a BREAKING NEWS banner across the screen, interrupting Barb "Hurricane" Smith's weather predictions. "This just in…" said the anchor.

"Dotty?"

"Quiet."

"The owner of an adult massage parlor…"

"Is there any other kind?"

"…was discovered dead in his apartment an hour ago, the victim of what appears to be strangulation. Lee Chen, age seventy-four…"

"What now, Dotty?"

"Hush, Naim."

"...a tenant, who called police. Police sought a suspect from the apartment building, who fled and escaped in a new model blue Mercedes..."

"Dotty! I thought you were in a taxi?"

"...suspect's name hasn't been released. We will have more, but now for our update with the sex party at the home of the Temple U lacrosse team." The anchor's face dissolved to a close-up of a beat reporter outside of the team's home holding a box of Lifestyle condoms.

'You didn't do him, did you?" Naim asked.

"No, I ain't been to Temple U in years."

"You know I am talking about Chen. You need to grow up."

"Some murdered named, Lynch, I been telling you about did the old man. The old bag from my building saw me moving the body."

"Oh, wow. Today?"

"A day ago, My bad, this just never came up in conversation."

"You're funny. What about the gigolo? He talking?"

Dotty scratched her left elbow. "You got Lysol around here. I need to get rid of these germs."

"No. Answer my question, Dotty."

She shrugged. "I'm not sure."

"This is crazy. How'd the hell you go from being a drunk detective—well, PI—to being involved in all of this?"

"I detect some shade in that comment, hun bun. Simple. A damn nun sewed her royal oats in a Mandingo warriors bed

THE DRUNK DETECTIVE

in my building. I got rid of her. Quietly, by the way. Now this Lynch clown wants to get rid of me, but Chen got in the damn way."

"Why not just tell the police all of this?"

"Too problematic. Chen was strangled in my apartment. I found him, and kindly took him to his place."

"Doesn't look good. But, hey, I'm just in law school."

"Who you telling?"

"You moved two dead bodies and told the police about neither. I mean, I am no lawyer, but my TV lawyer instincts are telling me you're in deep shit."

"Would you have told on yourself?"

"I'm a black ex-con with a rap sheet worthy of praise. Imagine it."

"Look, Butler, the bishop is dead, too. I'm pretty sure, Loretta Scalia sicced Lynch on Chen, Frankie and the bishop, but I don't know why. We will find out when you get into Scalia's computer."

"Let's do this," he said, looking at his watch. "It's that time. Wait here while I grab my car from the garage. Don't need anyone seeing you roaming the campus. They have that facial recognition crap included with the surveillance.

Just as Naim walked away, Dotty was approached by Hank Robinson.

"What are you doing here, Hankie Pankie?" she asked, fixing her hair.

"I should ask you that. I go to school here, remember?"

"Right. I found out some things about who may be responsible for hurting your brother. Turns out," she said, covering

her mouth, "well, I can't tell you right now, but I will say that there's a chance that DC is involved."

"Who's he?"

"The Government."

"Oh, Big Brother. That's fair, my brother hasn't filled out a W-2 in ages."

She giggled. "Ok, but this isn't about him not paying taxes in years. It could be apart of the problem, though." She heard a car horn and looked out and saw Naim waving at her. "I have to go."

"OK, but please find out who hurt my brother."

"I'll keep you posted."

"You have the Post-It already?" He smiled.

She blushed. "As a matter of fact, I do," she said, winked and then backed up. "I gotta run." She turned around and ran out of the building. Out of the corner of her eye she saw the Green Bay Packers jacket walking up the street. Someone pushing a shopping cart was wearing it.

Lightning Source UK Ltd.
Milton Keynes UK
UKHW01f1829040518
322147UK00001B/122/P